All Rights Reserved.
Copyright (c) 2015: R. Reese
1st Print 9/15

This work is of fiction. Names, characters, places images, and incidents, which are the product of the authors imagination used fictitiously. Any resemblance to actual persons or events is entirely coincidental. 'No part of this work may be reproduced or transmitted in any form or by any means without the written permission from the author.

To Order Books Contact:
PerpetualPenWritingGroup1@yahoo.com

ISBN- 9781517321321
ISBN-1517321328

Cover Design: Crystell Publications
Book Productions: Crystell Publications
We Help You Self Publish Your Book

Printed in the U.S.A.

Chapter 1

Filthy Snow

"Every time we come in here that hostess flirts with you! You tripping if you don't press on her ass!" Chuck taunted his close friend Jose.

They were in Hooters in South County, Missouri. Chuck stayed trying to put the jumper cables on somebody. The hostess he was referring to was a white babe who was extremely attractive. She was built up like a sister. Her round fat ass, thick thighs, and supple breasts were mouth watering. The fact that she happened to be white only made her that more desirable to darker suitors.

"You the one tripping man. You always talk that shit. If she is being nice it's because that is her job. That's all it is Chuck. Why don't you get at her since she so flirty?" Jose asked.

"There you go with all that! I'm telling you that she wants to fuck you dog! She is beyond friendly man! You sleeping on that snow bunny I tell you! I'm about to see what's up with her as soon as she walks past the table again! I bet she goes!"

"What you mean Chuck? I don't understand what you are trying to say here. Break shit down for me please and thank you."

"What I mean is I bet you that she gives up the pussy to one of us if not both! That's all I'm trying to say!"

"You always shooting your damn mouth off! What you betting big shot? Hmmm? I'm all ears!"

"I bet you $100! That is my bet right there! What you trying to do about it?"

"$100? I thought you believed in yourself a little more than that! I'll see your lil yard and raise this here pot to $250! You in or not?"

"$250? You trying to call my bluff huh? Well that shit won't work this time my dude! Why don't we throw a bottle of liquor in there to make it really interesting?"

"I think that we now have a bet!"

The hostess walked past their table. She was switching her nice ass that was crammed in her orange coochie cutter shorts. Chuck had to stop her.

"Hey! Excuse me! Excuse me!" Chuck said to get her attention.

"Yes? How may I help you? Is everything alright?" She said smiling.

"Yep. Everything is cool. I just wanted to tell you how sexy you were looking today."

"Why thank you sir. You are so kind."

"May I ask you your name? I don't want to rock the boat with you and your man though," Chuck said fishing.

"Well, I don't have a man. My name is Kirstie. I'm single all day every day," she laughed.

"I'm Chuck and this my boy Jose. Glad to know that you are single. Can you answer another question please?"

"As long as it's not too personal."

"It's not. I just wanted to know if you were interested in dating outside of your race."

"Hmmm. That's a great question right there. I'm from a very small town where they are extremely closed minded."

"Are you that way? Where you from exactly? If you don't mind me getting all up in your business once again."

"You guys ever heard of Red Bud, Il? No, I'm not prejudice. Not at all. I see no color regarding people. Does that answer your question or do you have more for me?"

"You still didn't answer my real question though."

"Oh? I didn't? I'm sorry. You can ask me again if you like."

"Do you mess with only white meat or do you prefer dark meat?"

"Hmm! Are you asking me if I date black guys? Is that what you are asking me?"

"That's exactly what I'm asking you."

"I wouldn't subject anyone to the racist shit in my town. They are still in the dark ages if you ask me. I would never parade around town with a black guy; but I would fuck him

5

behind closed doors. Now I don't want to come off as a slut, but that's my take on your question. You guys don't look at me like a whore do you? I feel so bad after saying what I just said to you guys! Oh my god!"

"Never apologize for being honest. It is how it is if you ask me. I appreciate your honesty."

She stood there for a while waiting for one of them to pull the trigger. No one stepped up so she prepared to step away from their table.

"Ok guys. I hope you are enjoying your meal here. I need to return to my post. Maybe we can chat later," she said smiling.

"Ok Kirstie. I appreciate you taking time out with us. Thank you. We will definitely holla at you in a few," Chuck assured her.

She waved as she walked off. They watched her with lust filled eyes.

"Damn man! She tough! Shit!" Jose proclaimed.

"I told you that she was gone go! You sitting there like a mute and shit! Fuck you thought?"

"Man what the hell are you talking about? You two had a conversation. You talking all that shit and she ain't went nowhere. We still sitting here dude. You sound crazy as hell!"

"You heard her! She ready to run out in rush hour traffic dog! You sitting right here while I'm making shit happen! I see I'm gone have to show you better than I tell you!"

"So far all you have showed me is a good talk game. That's all I'm seeing."

They finished their wings and fries. The waitress brought their check and the bill was settled along with a nice tip. They got up to leave, but not before stopping at the hostess station to pick at Kirstie one last time for the road. Chuck stepped right to her while Jose stood off to the side.

"We about to get on up out of here. I forgot to ask you if you any plans tonight. Hmmm?"

"Well I don't have any as of now. I'm probably gone see what my girl up to though."

"Oh? You got friends? Are they as fine as you?"

"Aww! You too sweet! My girlfriend is pretty attractive if you ask me. You would like her I'm sure," she laughed.

"Oh yeah? Why don't you give me your number so we can get up later on?"

"Here's my number. Make sure you call around 7 o'clock," she said handing him a piece of paper with her math attached.

"Yeah that is quite alright. I will make sure to call you. What ya'll gone be looking to get into later?"

"It's whatever. It don't really matter. What you got in your head right now?"

"You don't really want to know that! I'm telling you that right now for your own good! You'll get in trouble fucking with me!"

"What kind of trouble? Shit! If you got it like that, call me a daredevil!"

"Oh? You rolling like that? You ain't ready to get down and dirty for real! You better stop fronting!"

"Who fronting? Not me buddy! Try me if you think I'm a joke or something! You may just get the shock of your life!"

"You hear her talking all that shit dog? She don't realize she fucking with some real ones!"

"You the one doing all the talking! We from the show me state right? You don't have to chew my ear off! Just show me how real you are! You got the number! What you gone do with it?" Kirstie said strutting away from them.

All eyes were on her as she disappeared into the kitchen area. Chuck keyed the number into his cell phone quickly. He was too busy macking to notice that she already had her digits on the paper before being asked. A big smile covered his face while saving her contact info.

"Now you see that? You were on the front row watching the show! Hope you don't have nothing to do later on. Looks like we flipping another episode tonight! You up for it?"

"I'm cool with whatever. That's a thick white piece right there! Sheesh!" Jose said.

"Oh hell naw! Don't be eyeing my white bitch! I got plans for her thick ass! She gone feel the fire in a little while!"

"Yeah I hear you. Hope you know what to do with her. Don't be just blowing hot air! She a nice piece alright."

They went back and forth all the way to the car. The seeds had been planted and were sure to sprout more sooner than later. They rode around the city streets to pass time. Chuck was thinking about the nice piece of white meat he was on the verge of slaying. His grin let you know what was on his mind. Jose was nodding his head to some music he had playing on his cell phone.

"You better hope her friend just as decent as she is man. She gone get this work regardless! Mark my words! You about to lose this bet!"

"There you go talking loud again. You just love hearing yourself huh? I'm just chilling back until then. Matter of fact, you should be getting ready to call her now. We can put the bullshit to rest soon enough. Gone make the call! What you waiting on?" Jose snapped.

"You sound like you been sipping on some crazy juice! Let me find out you sleeping with your eyes open! Call being made right now! Sit back and take notes! You need a pen or pencil?" Chuck laughed.

"I got my pen and paper in hand! Just make the call already!"

Chuck dialed the number and waited for an answer. After a few rings someone picked up.

"Hello? Who is this?" Kirstie asked.

"This Chuck baby. We met earlier at your job. Don't tell me you done forgot about me already!"

"Oh! Sorry about that! How are you?"

"I'm cool baby. What's up for tonight?"

"I haven't the slightest idea. We're trying to figure it out now. What's going on?"

"For real? Me and my buddy want to get into something."

"Something like what?" Kirstie giggled.

"It doesn't matter for real. I'm open to any and all suggestions."

"We don't want to go out. We just want to chill. We can drink, smoke, or whatever."

Chuck gave Jose the thumbs up sign. The green light had indeed been activated. Jose's face lit up once he was aware of the situation. The ball was bouncing in their court now.

"So ya'll just want to get fucked up huh?"

"It doesn't matter to us at all. Whatever you throw at us we gone catch it!"

"You need to be very careful how you putting that thang out there! Me and my guy with the shit all day every day! What time do you have to be back in Red Bud? Don't want to get no one in trouble!" Chuck smirked.

"Who gone get in trouble? My man works at Granite City Steel so I have plenty free time to do whatever the fuck I want! I have to work early in the morning, but we can hang all night if your girlfriend doesn't mind! Don't want to get you in hot water either! I'm trying to look out for you as well!" Kirstie jabbed back.

"I keep my bitch in line thank you very much! We can kick it all night! You gone fuck around and get yourself in some deep shit! We plays no games around here! You hear me?"

"Oh yeah! I'm shaking in my boots! You got me second guessing this whole situation right now!"

Chuck didn't appreciate her sarcasm so he decided to crank it up a few more notches.

"You better be thinking cause we having a lock in up in this bitch tonight!"

"A lock in? Please explain what that is."

"A lock in is when you and some other people all get on one side of the door. You lock it tight and whatever happens happens."

"So you can't leave when you want to? That's a bummer!"

"You won't be held against your will if that is what you are worried about. We are all grown and can leave at any time. Let's just be clear on that."

"I never heard of a lock in where you could go back and forth once the door is locked. Hmmm. Sounds pretty lame if you ask me," Kirstie said.

"Lame? There ain't shit lame about us! You got us fucked up for real baby!"

Kirstie observed how easy she could tick Chuck off. She made note to use that to her advantage in the future.

"Calm down honey lump! You getting all worked up for nothing. Relax baby. I know East St. Louis is no joke. All I'm saying is that you should be more direct in your lock up deal or whatever."

"What do you mean by that?"

Chuck switched the phone over to loud speaker. Jose was listening and being quiet until he heard their last exchange.

"Aye! What she means is you need to say what you mean and mean what you say! Tell her how you really feel dog!" Jose said in a hushed voice.

"Oh for real? Just lay it out there huh?" Chuck said amped.

Jose nodded his head to let him know that he was on the right track. They shared evil grins as he got back to the conversation.

"It's a lock in dear! Once you there you there! Bring everything you gone need cause it's no turning back once them doors lock! The doors will be on time sensitive locks that won't open until the sun comes up! What happens during the lock in is grown folks business!"

"That sounds like it may be worth checking out for real. Hmmmm! You got rubbers?"

"Nope."

"I'll bring some. Do you have something to drink?"

"Not for real. You can bring that too. What were you thinking about getting?"

"I'm thinking about Everclear shots and juice hook ups."

"Damn! Everclear? That shit can start your car!"

"Now don't tell me you scared! That happens to be our shit!"

"Yeah I guess we can fuck with it. Ain't nothing to it but to do it! Fuck it! Bring it on then!"

"Ok. We will definitely do that. What time you talking about getting together? Where we doing this at?"

"Ummm we ready now! We over off 62nd and Lake Drive."

"You right off the main drag huh? I got it. We'll be through in the next hour or so. Is that cool? We'll have the dick rubbers and the alcohol. Is there anything else you want before we get there?"

Another dumb grin marked Chuck's face. He was delighted at their generosity. His thirsty ass took full advantage.

"Why don't you get us some Taco Bell? That 12 box will do the trick!"

"What kind of sauce do you want honey?"

"Get a little bit of everything if you don't mind. Don't forget the napkins."

"I got you. I'll give you a ring once we're in your area. See you in a few."

"Ok baby. Get here as soon as you can. We'll be waiting."

"Sounds cool. Oh yeah! Before I go I need to ask you a question."

"Ok. I'm all ears."

"You two are the only ones there right? I mean we don't want any surprises. You feel me?"

"Naw baby. We the only two here and that will remain that way until you get here."

"Huh? Why you say that? Explain please."

"It's only two of us here. When you come through the number will change to four. You got it?"

"Yeah I got it. Thanks for clearing that up for me. I hate misunderstandings. Don't you?"

"I sure do. Ok see you soon."

"Ok honey."

They hung up and the guys got to cleaning up the house. That only meant that they just threw shit out of sight so the ladies wouldn't notice. The ladies were also getting ready for the evening. Kirstie picked up her friend Mallory who was short and on the thick end of the spectrum. Her pretty face was adorned with long auburn hair pulled into a pony tail. Her breasts were larger than normal which caught your attention right away. She also had an ass on her that made her even more desirable to the brothers. These were too cornbread fed snow bunnies who had no interest in men of their same race. They were more partial to the darker meat if you know what I mean.

"You got condoms bitch?" Kirstie asked.

"I sure do! I got about a dozen! Don't worry! We are more than covered on that end! We still have to get the liquor don't we?" Mallory asked.

"I already got it on my way home from work. All we got to do is get these guys some tacos."

"What did you get to drink Kirstie?"

"You know what we like to drink when we party!"Kirstie said pulling the bottle out the bag.

"Oh shit! It's about to be so on! Oh my freaking god! You not playing huh?"

"We are fixing to handle some real serious business here! What were you thinking?"

"How does his friend look?"

"He's decent looking. He appears to be clean. He seems like a nice guy. You'll like him once you see him. If you don't, you can holla at the other guy. You know it don't matter to me. It's whatever!"

"There go your crazy self talking all slick and shit! It don't matter to me either! We can fuck and switch as far as I'm concerned! You know how we do what we do!"

They slapped hands as they rode to Taco Bell off highway 157 in Caseyville, IL. They ordered their food and were en route to Lake Drive. Kirstie called Chuck for the address. Chuck gave her the info and they found him in a matter of minutes.

"Oh shit dog! They outside right now! Her partner nice and juicy too! Damn! Look like you came up dog! Shit! I want the other one! Wonder if it's too late to switch horses?"

"First you digging on old girl! Now you want the friend! Shit! Make up your mind man! They both decent to me. I'll take either one! I'm open to whatever! How about you just take them both since you can't decide? I'm far from a hater!"

The girls made it to the front door of the house. Before they rang the doorbell, the door flew open with both guys cheesing like crazy.

"Hey ladies! How is it going?" Chuck said.

"Let me get them bags. Don't need ya'll straining your pretty little bodies," Jose offered.

"I see gentleman still exist. I'll have to mark this down on my calendar. It ain't everyday that someone treats you nice. Why thank you kind sir! Kirstie said sincerely.

"Hmmm! I like that! You starting shit off right! You gone spoil us rotten!" Mallory added.

Jose winked his eye at Chuck who was too busy lusting over the white meat in his presence.

"Ya'll can sit here," Jose said directing them to the couch.

Chuck went through the bag with the alcohol in it. Jose put the bag of ice in the freezer. Chuck started to dig in the box of tacos.

"Damn man! You not gone wash your hands? Come on now homeboy!" Jose scolded his overzealous partner.

The girls looked on as the guys talked at the table. They didn't offer their two cents. They simply sat there quietly.

"Hey! Ya'll want something to eat? I mean, it's plenty thanks to you two," Jose said.

"Damn man! It's only just enough for the two of us! Goddamn!" Chuck complained as if he bought the food.

"Man chill out! You tripping!" Jose said kicking him under the table.

"It's ok. We already ate before we came anyway. We appreciate the offer though," Kirstie said.

"I was just making sure ya'll was cool. It's only right," Jose smirked.

Jose was charming while Chuck was offensive. Chuck dug into his food and started smacking loudly. Jose just shook his head.

"Damn! I see ya'll brought some hard shit!" Jose stated.

"That's not even hard for real. It's pretty normal where we come from baby. Don't tell me you can't hang!" Mallory asked laughing.

"He don't look like a lightweight to me girl. I think he can hang," Kirstie chimed in.

"Ain't no lightweight shit over this way! You gone see soon enough! I ain't got to talk your ears off!" Chuck said chewing with his mouth wide open.

"You mind if we fix our drinks or do you want us to wait until you are finished eating? It doesn't matter to us for real," Kirstie said.

"Gone knock yourself out. It's all good in the hood! Mi casa es su casa!" Chuck said.

"Don't mind if we do!"

The girls went in the kitchen to do their thing. They took the plastic cups from the bag and began to pour. They walked back into the room with their drinks in hand. The guys couldn't help but notice how clear their beverages were.

"What ya'll mix it with? Must be white soda or something," Chuck inquired.

They laughed at his comments.

"Naw honey. This just some good old fashioned ice and drank right here. Nothing more nothing less," Mallory said.

When they were finished eating, they threw their garbage away. Then they prepared their drinks carefully. Jose held the bottle up and smiled.

"Shit can't do nothing but get out of hand dog. Them gals drinking this shit on the rocks like it's nothing," Jose said.

"I'm about to get my drink on just like ya'll! This ain't nothing but white liquor! All this shit the same in my book! I drink dark myself, but in this case I'll make an exception," Chuck bragged.

"Man you might want to cut it a lil bit. This shit strong like a bull on steroids! You have to respect this here dog!" Jose said fixing his drink.

He made sure to dilute it to his standards. He knew better. White chicks can drink like there is no tomorrow. Chuck always threw caution to the wind and was sure to crash and burn very soon.

"You sound like an amateur or something! You can't even handle your alcohol huh? Is that what you are saying to me? Let me find out that you can't hang for real!"

"Never soft my dude! I'm just trying to look out for your best interest. It's all good and you a grown ass man at the end of the day!"

"Yeah that's what I thought! Stay in your lane man! We on some grown folk shit right now! Either you in or you not!"

They finished preparing their drinks and walked into the area where the girls were. The ladies had already put away half of what was in their cups. The guys peeped that and the excitement level rose.

"I see ya'll done started without us!" Jose joked.

"Oh no sweetie! We just sipping and what not. I do have a question though," Mallory said.

"What's that sweet cheeks? Ask whatever you want to!" Chuck said.

"This is supposed to be a lock in right? I mean that is what you said earlier right?" Kirstie asked.

"Why yes! This is indeed a lock in! What are we missing? Please tell me!" Chuck said grinning.

Kirstie smiled as she rose from the couch. She walked to the windows and closed the blinds. Then she locked all the locks on the front door. She turned and looked at them and gave them a wink.

"Now I think this qualifies as an official lock in! Everything is now safe and secure!" Kirstie said.

The guys started to rub their hands together. Things were now moving in a promising direction. Chuck began caressing the ever growing bulge hiding in his pants. Mallory noticed and licked her lips. His gesture made her a little hot and horny.

"Mmmmm! I see you grabbing on that cock! What you plan on doing with it?" Mallory asked.

"What you got in mind? We need to know!" Jose said.

Everybody was drinking and feeling fine. Mallory dumped the condoms on the table.

"We got condoms and this here for an even better time!" She said holding up a fresh tube of lube.

The guys looked at one another and back at the ladies. More sips were taken from their cups.

"What's the lube for? Your pussies must don't get wet huh? Damn!" Chuck cackled.

"Never! You can check for yourself if you doubt me!" Kirstie said.

She undid her pants to expose her cotton underwear with hearts all over them. She proceeded to take her shit off. She was now naked from the waist down. Her vagina was devoid of any hair. She walked over to Chuck. She placed his hand on her pussy in order for him to test the wetness factor. He immediately began finger banging her box. Mallory had a heat index level that was steadily rising. She began to rub her fat titties through her shirt. Kirstie took Chuck's finger out of her snatch and put it in her mouth. His dick damn near busted through his pants. Kirstie looked at his growing bulge.

"Mmm! I see someone is excited! Is that a sock or all you? Let me see that fucking cock!" Mallory insisted.

"Not before I see what you working with! What's up ladies?" Chuck asked.

Kirstie peeled off her pants but kept on her sneakers. Chuck looked at her with a strange eye of sorts. He keyed in on her lower body which was on full display.

"Could you turn around for me so I can see that ass?" He ordered.

She spun around and bent over. She took both hands and parted her butt cheeks clean apart. She made her asshole pulse in and out like a heartbeat. The guys both moved in closer to see the action. Jose began to grow in his trousers as well.

"That looks like it's trying to tell me something. Huh? I can't hear you?" Jose spoke to her anus.

Jose took his tongue and swiped it across her exposed bung hole. He grabbed one of her cheeks for better access.

"Mmm! Damn baby! I can't be mad at you! You getting right to the point huh?" Kirstie asked.

Chuck sat there stunned at Jose's behavior. He also was getting a little jealous. Jose was living in the moment. Mallory was impressed at the take charge approach that Jose displayed. After a few intense moments of ass eating, he pulled his tongue out her asshole.

"You good Ma? That was just a warm up! We about to kick this bitch off the right way! Stay tuned!" Jose said as he made his way to the kitchen.

Chuck followed in behind him. Jose fixed another drink and took a sip.

"Man you a wild motherfucker! You just gone eat the white bitch ass in front of us? What the fuck man! That bitch still wearing them beat up ass tennis shoes! You really tripping dude! You ain't got no chill huh? I thought you was gone whip your cock out and slay the broad! You still drinking that gasoline ass shit?"

Jose was losing respect for his friend by the second.

"Man what the fuck is your problem? We got two pieces of ready to serve white pussy and all you can do is watch what I'm doing!"

"I'm just saying bro. I can't believe what you just did man! You crazy as fuck dog! You just don't give a fuck do you?"

Jose drank and listened. He could not believe what he was hearing. He thought his buddy was a player, but clearly that was not the case!

"Yo dog let's just get loose with the pink toes! I'm not trying to hear nothing you talking about! I'm about to gone back in there and partake in a little adult action! I don't give a shit what they shoes look like! I'm not trying to fuck they shoes no way!" Jose said.

Chuck looked dumb as hell. He could not begin to understand Jose's attitude. He just didn't get it. He grimaced at the taste of the potent liquor. Even though they applied a mixing agent, that shit was still strong. He watched Jose go back in to join the ladies. Jose acted right at home with them. That made Chuck's insecurities bubble to the surface on the low.

"You ladies in need of a refresher? I'll get it for you if you want me to," Jose offered smiling.

"You see that? He is definitely a real gentleman! Yes please get us more alcohol! What's the deal with your friend? He needs to take some notes from you," Mallory asked jokingly.

Chuck overheard her comments and flew out the kitchen to confront her, "I need to take notes? Da fuck does that mean? Ya'll not feeling me or something?"

"Whoa! Don't get all antsy now dude. I'm just saying that it's cool to treat people nice. That's all I'm saying! I don't want any problems with you!" Mallory said.

"I am being nice! Ya'll can't tell? I'm the one that got this lock in on and popping!" Chuck protested.

"Yes you did, but did you know that females will be more inclined to please and cater to you if you are nice to them? You ever heard of the vinegar and honey scenario? Hmmm? How you gone get your dick sucked if you can't be nice?" Mallory said with a sly wink.

"Oh yeah? It's like that huh? You making me see things the way you trying to put them! I'll try and be nice from now on!" Chuck said holding his wood through his pants.

They were attempting to set the stage/mood if Chuck would just shut the fuck up and flow with it. Mallory removed the rest of Kirstie's clothes. She was just as thick naked and the guys were far from disappointed. Chuck lusted over Kirstie as she stood there in all her glory. Jose took a sip from his cup before getting back to his ass eating venture.

"Oh shit now boo! That fucking tongue is right up my ass! Mmm! You really know how to make a gal feel wanted!" Kirstie moaned.

"You feel my tongue in your asshole baby? I want you to feel me as I taste you! This ass tastes good too!" Jose said while feasting on her sweet ass.

Chuck stood there dumbfounded. Jose was too busy doing his thing to notice who was watching him. He buried his face even farther up her ass. Mallory was feeling left out due to Chuck's inactivity. She eyed Chuck who was just standing there. She walked over and started to undo his pants. She pulled his cock out and got to sucking him off. He leaned against the wall and watched her go to town on his member. Everyone was clearly occupied. The lock in was now underway!

"Mmm! Suck this dick hoe! You better suck it like you mean it! Yeah! Just like that! Shit!"

Chuck gripped her ass as she blew him lovely. He could see her ass as her underwear inched down. She took the hint and pulled her pants off so he could see her goods. Mallory still had on her sneakers.

"Oh baby! Your cock is tasty! I can't stop licking on this black dick! Mmmm! Damn! You liking this? Call me your dirty white bitch!" Mallory requested before burying his manhood deep down her throat.

"Fuck yeah! I hear you dirty white bitch! You better suck them balls too! My balls better not be dry and lonely you dirty white slut you!"

"That's the shit I like right there! Slap me in the face with your fucking dick! Shit feels so killer when a big black cock smacks my face! Mmmm yeah!"

Chuck followed her instructions. The more he slapped dick to her face, the more intense her sucking became. He could barely concentrate on the matter before him because he was too worried about who was paying attention to him. He wanted to watch everyone but didn't want anyone to see what he was doing. Kirstie and Jose were too deep off in their own bag to notice what anyone else had going on. Kirstie rubbed her clit intensely as Jose went from her asshole to her pussy hole and back again. His enthusiasm was driving her up the walls.

"Mmm! Goddamn baby! You sure do know your way around back there! Don't stop! You been holding out on me huh? Don't you fucking stop!" Kirstie moaned.

She was on her knees on the couch with Jose's face square in her pasty ass crack. He was going to town and didn't give two shits about who knew it.

"You like it huh? This white pussy tastes so fucking good! This white ass not short stopping either!" Jose said unplugging his face from her anal crevice.

Chuck and Mallory were in the corner getting busy as well. She was being dick slapped and loving every minute of it. She took her panties off with his cock resting snugly in her mouth.

"Wait a minute baby. Let me go to the restroom for a quick second please," Mallory said.

"It's down the hall on your right. The door is open with the light on," Chuck told her.

Mallory walked to the bathroom in nothing but her sneakers. He watched her odd shaped ass jiggle away. He kept his eyes on the other two as well. He covered his dick with his hand as he inched over to get a closer look. Their backs were turned so they didn't know what he was doing. He eased back into the corner and stepped on Mallory's underwear on the floor. He looked closer at them to see colored stains decorating the crotch area. Anybody else would've been disgusted at the sight. Chuck wasn't even tripping. He heard the toilet flush and she came out the bathroom. No water was heard other than the toilet, so it was clear that she skipped the washing hands part. Chuck walked in after her to take a piss. The odor in there was not present before. He smelled it and kept it moving. She was waiting on him once he came out. She hugged him around his neck and kissed him before going down his chest and back to his cock once again.

"Let's go into the bedroom so we can really get wild baby! Is that cool with you?" Chuck asked.

She nodded yes with his cock still between her jaws. She kept it there as they shuffled to the killing floor. It takes great skill to walk with your dick lodged in a chick's mouth. At least that's what I hear! They got to the room and there was only a dirty mattress on the floor. She pushed Chuck and he fell onto it backwards. His cock slammed against his stomach upon impact.

"Mmm! I got you now boo! Don't you worry about shit! Let me get my drink from the other room baby. I'll be right on back before you can miss me," Mallory assured him.

She walked to the toilet to relieve herself again before getting her drink. Jose and Kirstie were in full swing at this point. Kirstie was sucking him off as his eyes danced around the back of his head. Mallory searched for her cup among the others on the table. No one marked theirs so she had her work cut out. She took a sip out of every cup trying to see which was hers.

Anyone with half a brain would've just made a new drink, but not her. She made up her mind after she tasted the last one. She then took her cup and added more alcohol to it. She walked her naked ass back the room where Chuck was waiting. As soon as she shut the door, he was all over her. He pinned her up against the wall before kissing her open mouth. He moved on to her sweaty neck and on down to her salty breasts. The taste from her body fucked with him, but hardly enough to halt his trip down to her vagina. He noticed a faint odor, but paid it no mind. Mallory drank while he covered her body with sloppy kisses.

"Let me get some of that liquor if you don't mind," he asked in an effort to wash the gritty taste from his mouth.

"Here you go. Take it easy. I didn't put nothing in it but ice," she forewarned.

"Yeah ok! It's nothing to a giant! I got this!" Chuck boasted as he guzzled the pure alcohol.

He handed her the cup before getting back to business. Her smell invaded his nose as he made his way down her happy trail. Her pussy was bald so he got right on her clit.

"Ahhh! Mmmmm! Shit boo! Ahhh!" Mallory moaned.

He licked her clit side to side then up and down. She took her fingers and opened her pink pussy lips as far as they could go. Now he was dealing with her cat up close and very personal. He shifted his busy tongue over to her open twat. The aroma emitted from her vagina proudly. He closed his eyes as he lapped from her glory hole. He scrunched his face up as the smell and taste double teamed his nose and mouth. He held his breath as he fucked her with his tongue. Her pussy reminded him of a pissy sponge. The scent was no better either. It took no time in making its presence very well known in the room. She sipped her potion not giving a fuck that her personal hygiene was a fucking mess. Chuck had to drink in order to replace the piss taste. He kept closing his eyes while lying to himself about what he was actually tasting. Mallory gripped the back of his head and forced his face into her smelly coochie.

"Eat that fucking pink pussy baby! Mmmm! That tongue feels lovely on my fucking clit! Keep it right there!" Mallory begged.

It was difficult for Chuck to respond so he let his tongue do the talking. He continued to chow down in between her legs. His hard work was about to pay off. She was about to blow her top in record time.

"Aah shit boo! You eating my cunt so good right now! Lick it! Lick it faster! Holy fuck! Fuuuuucckkk!" She said while erupting in his mouth.

Chuck frowned as her sour creamy scented discharge left her honey hole. He kept on eating as shit oozed down his chin. He turned her over on her side and parted her ass cheeks. The smell of an old fart wafted in the air as he dived in. He tilted his head back so the stench would not over take him. He caught his breath before eating her ass. As he moved closer to his target, he saw crusty shit crumbs that were gathered around her asshole. The sight of this did nothing to deter his mission. He spreaded her anal passage farther to give it that open eye effect. He took another drink and by this time, he was even more buzzed. He eased his tongue right up her ass.

"Oooh shit! You eating my ass huh baby? Fuck! That feels good! Goddamn! Fuck my ass with that fucking tongue! You know how to use that mufucka huh?" Mallory egged him on.

Chuck dined on her ass like it was his last meal. He inserted two fingers into her pussy and it only drove her closer to the edge.

"Fuck boo! You know you doing your thang down there ain't you? Fuck my ass with your tongue! Finger bang this pussy! Put another one in there too baby! Shit! I ain't scared boo!"

Chuck worked her while she sucked her own tits. The sight only made him finger fuck her faster. He continued to devour her anus like the nasty motherfucker that he really was.

"Boo I'm ready to fuck you now! You wanna fuck me boo? You ready for this?"

Chuck heard this and rose right on up. He smiled at her with his shit eating grin. Mallory left the room to get a fresh drink and the condoms. She came back and threw them on the mattress along with the lube. Chuck immediately picked it up before giving Mallory the raised eyebrow look. He knew what it was, but he had to verify with her first.

"Mmph! What do you have here? This is what I think it is?"

"Is there a problem? You ain't scared are you? She said with a wink.

"Your pussy seems wet enough to me!"

She shook her head at his last statement. Chuck was totally oblivious to what she was getting at. She was going to have to give him a crash course immediately so they could be on the exact same page once and for all.

"Boo this ain't for my pussy. My pussy is wet as the Mississippi River baby! You see what I'm working with! This is for my ass."

"Oh! I knew that! I was just fucking with you! I know what's up!" Chuck said faking his ass off.

Mallory twisted her lips as she shook her head. She played with her twat as Chuck awaited her next move. She did not disappoint him at all either. She rested on her back and hiked her legs wide and high in the air. The discharge seeped from her crotch and into her anal area. It formed an interesting sticky mass. She took one last drink before sitting her cup on the floor. Chuck picked the cup up and drank from it also. You could hear Kirstie screaming from the other room. They listened as she waited for Chuck to apply the lube.

"I hear someone enjoying themselves! You better come on before I get jealous!" She teased.

She let out a fart as the lube touched her butt hole. Chuck ignored the smell that came with it. The foul odor in the room overpowered whatever that came afterward. He rubbed the ass grease in with his finger. He didn't give a damn that her ass was turning his finger brown.

"Is that enough lube for you or do you need more? It's plenty left."

"It's your call baby. I don't know what you are comfortable with. As long as you can get that cock in my ass I'm not complaining. Hurry up and give me that dick! Come on!" Mallory begged.

"Mmm! I got this! Let me do what I need to do! You gone feel me soon enough! You got me hard as fuck!"

Chuck had her slippery as hell. He probed her with two fingers in order to loosen her up. He worked her until he felt that she was ready for takeoff.

"You ready?"

Mallory put her legs as far back as she could get them. She resembled a human pretzel. She stared at Chuck with inviting eyes.

"I hope this answers any questions you may have for me," she teased.

Chuck stroked his meat as he prepared to enter her dirty backdoor. There were condoms available, but he looked right past them. He took his naked dick and rubbed it against her pussy. He squirted lube on his man as he jacked it.

"You gone tease me or please me with your black cock? What's up? You ready for this here or what? Come on baby!"

"I been ready! Ease on down here a lil bit baby."

"Ok baby. I got you," Mallory said.

She scooted closer to his waiting dick. He rotated his stiff rod against her glazed anus. It throbbed in and out at the first touch of his penis. He stuck three fingers in and pulled them out. He then took his dick and pressed the head into her ass with his thumb. She didn't blink as his dick head disappeared up her rectum.

"Oh yeah! Feels good baby! Put that dick all the way in my ass! Give it to me! Shit!"

Chuck followed her orders. He pushed deeper into her dooky hole. He was halfway there before he decided to just barge on in.

"Oooh! Fuck me! Your dick belongs to my asshole now! Don't you dare stop fucking me until I tell you to!"

Chuck was too busy fucking to answer any questions. Her asshole held onto his dick for dear life. He worked his number as she held her legs back. Her eyes rolled around in her head before she set them on him. She flicked her tongue at him. He got the message and leaned in to kiss her. The foulness of her breath invaded his mouth. He ignored it and kissed her even harder.

"You like my ass on your cock baby? You fucking me so good!" Mallory said in between smooches.

Chuck bore down during their slow grind. He put his head over her shoulder and into the filthy mattress. He did his best to concentrate. Her tight ass would force him to tap out early if he wasn't careful. The more he stroked, the wetter and sloppier her ass seemed to become. The Everclear was taking effect on him slowly but surely. It was starting to become next to impossible for his vision to remain clear. The room started to rotate and he tried his best to keep it together. Mallory squirmed under him as his dick invaded her asshole.

"Goddamn baby! I'm about to cum!"

"I didn't know your ass could cum baby. That's new to me."

Mallory just laughed, "Nawl boo. You fucking my ass makes my pussy cum."

"Just keep them legs back for me. I like that shit."

Mallory took her legs and put them in the formation of a letter Y. She raised her head up so she could get a view of the action. The dick to asshole scenario was unreal. Chuck was mesmerized.

"You like what you see baby? Oh God!"

There was more discharge coming from her vagina. It was thick and covering her ass crack. Chuck closed his eyes and breathed in deep. The mixture of ass, shit, funky breath, body odor, piss, and sour pussy hole quietly filled the room. They probably confused it with sex, but that shit wasn't right at all. He pumped away at her shit box nevertheless. The muddy secretion coated his dick like a burgundy condom. He kissed her lips once more as the shit was getting good to him. The room began to pick up speed on him. Mallory shifted to her side. Now her legs were in an L formation. She took her elevated leg and stretched it back. Her free hand fondled her pussy while the dick stabbed her asshole. The liquor had Chuck leaning in to kiss her mouth. They touched tongues as they lip locked. Her leg rested on his shoulder the whole time. He was making love to her. Jose walked by the door and stuck his head in to see what was up. He hurried and shut the door once that smell hit him.

"Goddamn! Somebody done died up in there! Shit!" He said to himself.

Chuck looked up at what he thought he just heard. When he didn't see anyone, he put his head back down.

"Damn baby. Did you hear something?"

"Huh?"

"I could've sworn I just heard something. You didn't hear nothing?"

"I ain't hear shit! Keep fucking me! That's all you should be trying to hear!"

"I see you got jokes. This ass feels so good! Mmm! I like how you finger fucking that fat pussy too!"

"You like that ass huh? Taste my cunt then! Here you go!" Mallory said shoving her sticky fingers in his mouth.

He screwed up his face as he realized what was going on. He gagged as he swallowed her juices. She pulled him in for another open mouth kiss. She tasted herself by way of his lips.

"My shit tastes good huh? Fuck my ass! You all up in me baby! Mmmm!"

Chuck listened as he fucked her slow. She ran her finger down his chest and played with his pubic hairs. She massaged his dick as it ran in and out of her. That drove him closer to his breaking point. Mallory looked in his eyes while gritting her teeth.

"Bring that dick to me baby!" She commanded.

"You mean right now? I'm not fixing to bust yet!"

"I don't give a fuck! Remove your cock from my ass and place it down my throat please! Come on baby! I want to suck you real quick! Give it to me! Fuck my face please!"
He backed out of her shit box and straddled her chest. Mallory took her breasts and rubbed them against his ready penis.
"Fuck my tits first! Mmm! I love that shit!"
Chuck moved his hips back and forth in between her large melons. She spit on it as it peeped out the other side of her boobs. She also sucked and licked on him to intensify the action. Their eyes locked as his cock popped in and out of her tits and mouth. Even though there was all sorts of fecal matter/vagina discharge dripping from him, she had no problem accepting him into her mouth.
"Yeah suck this dick! Mmm!"
He titty banged her with precision. He rested against the wall as his head spun out of control. His blurred vision was fuzzy as shit. Mallory sucked him like a wild animal. Her mouth was waiting every time his dick poked through her tits. He loved the attention his cock was getting. Chuck was starting to miss her warm asshole. That sucking shit was getting old fast.
"I'm ready to fuck some more! You got that?"
"You want to fill my asshole up with your big black dick? Is that what you want? Hmmm? Tell me baby cause that makes me so fucking wet! Talk to me!"
Without any warning, Chuck called up Earl and tossed his cookies all upside the wall. Some of it landed in her hair. It

did nothing to stop the blowjob that she was currently performing.

"Baby are you alright? You need to stop or something to get yourself together?"

"I'm good. It's just something fucking with my stomach. I'm good though. Let's keep this going."

Chuck was feeling like a light weight. He did his best to save face, but he knew he had fucked up the flow. He pulled out her mouth and moved back down to her butt. He was having a hard time lining up his cock to her waiting brown eye. She noticed and helped him out some.

"Damn! I'm buzzing like a fool right now! Shit got me out there for real!"

"I see. Let me give you a hand there. Hold still baby. This dick has to get back in my asshole! Fuck! We almost got it baby!"

As she tried to plug him into her anal socket, the room began to spin even faster for Chuck. His head got lighter as he inched closer to the blackout zone. Without any warning, he fell backwards onto the scummy mattress.

"What the hell?" Mallory said looking back.

He was out cold, but his jimmy was still wide awake. She didn't hesitate to straddle him. She put a hand on his chest and guided him into her anus with the other hand. Before long, she was sitting squarely on his cock.

"Ummmm! Aaaah! Mmmm!" She moaned.

She kissed him and tried to wake him up with no luck. He was not coming to anytime soon. Once she realized this, she went wild on him until she got her proper fill of penis. She bounced up and down on him until she reached her pressure point.

"Aaah daddy! I'm about to cream all over you and this good cock! You hear me baby? Hmmm! Mmmm! Your cock is so fucking hard right now! Fuck baby!"

Chuck lay there comatose unaware that he was getting the shit fucked out of him. Mallory bucked on him until she exploded.

"Goddamn! Shit! You just made my day without even knowing it! Good looking baby," she said kissing his open mouth.

She didn't even get up to wash herself off. She stayed on top of him and went to sleep with his shank still wedged between her messy butt cheeks. The rest of the night slipped away as they both slept. The morning came with Chuck still being out cold. Mallory was gone. Footsteps could be heard coming towards the door. The knob turned and the door opened. Chuck still hadn't budged.

"Dawg! Wake your ass up man! Ya'll fucked this shit up in here huh dawg? Goddamn! What the fuck going on? Get your ass up!" Jose yelled as he kicked the filthy mattress.

"Huh? What's up?"

"Man get your ass up and clean this shit up! You really fucked this bitch up! Goddamn!" Jose complained.

"I'll be up in a minute. Give me some time to get it together," Chuck said rising up for the first time of the day.

"You a real nasty dude boy! Look at this bullshit!" Jose said leaving out the door.

Chuck rubbed his head as he looked around the room. The vomit decorated the floor and wall. There was feces on the mattress as well as all over his dick and legs. The room smelled like a portable toilet that was out of order.

"I'll deal with this when I get up. Fuck it!" Chuck said before dozing back off.

He shook his head and laid back down in the vomit and shit infested room.

Chapter 2

Gamers

"I got next on that Call of Duty! Niggas know what it is! Old fag ass niggas can't fuck with me!" Bee declared.

"Man fuck this game! Where the bitches? It's way too many niggas up in here!" Tez pointed out.

The trap house/club house was flooded with dudes. They were drinking, smoking, and gambling on the video game. A few cats were catching a few plays here and there. Gucci Mane was blasting on the system. Some of the niggas rapped along with the music. There was a dice game taking place in the corner of the room.

"These old faggot ass niggas don't know shit about no mufucking dice! Fuck ya'll doing over here? Ain't too much bread on the floor so I guess ya'll just on some practice shit!"

"Bee you need to chill on calling everybody out they name. Shit ain't cool bro. You don't like being called nothing but your name dude. Give people respect man," Tez spoke up.

Everybody kind of nodded their heads in agreement. Bee had a bad habit of calling everyone homosexuals. He was a so-called tough guy who had seen and survived his share of drama. He went to prison and was shot several times. He was short and stocky. He was also as mean as a rattlesnake on its period. He was brown skinned with waves smothering the crown of his head. He worked out and ate right. He just couldn't get his mind right. He fancied pills, codeine, alcohol, and plenty of top shelf reefer. He was the big mouth of the trap, but he was also pretty decent with his hands. That was foreign to the younger cats that frequented the trap. They preferred side arms with long ass extended clips.

"Chill out Tez. You act like you some player ass nigga or something. Always talking about some sorry ass hoes."

"Man gone head with that bullshit! You stay on some other shit! I'm ready to see some hoes! Niggas can't do nothing for me man! Let me see what's what for today," Tez said texting on his phone.

"Ya'll know this the trap! We got the game jumping off! I got money on the wood!" Bee said.

More weed was rolled as the shit kept getting kicked around. They were playing online with some real disrespectful people. In the heat of gambling, anything goes. You see a whole different man once that money on the line. Guys began to slowly dissolve from the house as their money dwindled.

"All these fags leaving? Thought ya'll money was as big as ya'll mouths? Get the fuck outta here! We big boys around here! Maybe you need to go hit your stash and come on back! If ya'll want to double back, I'm taking on all comers! Faggot ass niggas gone have to come better next time!"

"I understand you feeling yourself and all, but goddamn man. Your mouth crazy reckless. You in a room full of men bro. Ain't no punks, fags, or sissies here. You should slow down on all that sweet nigga talk man," the lil homie Jay spoke up.

"Man ain't nobody trying to hear no shit from your ass Jay! You just hot cause you popped on the dice and the game! It ain't my fault your skills not up to par! Your lil ass better go home and practice! That's what you need to be doing instead of trying to fake check me!" Bee countered.

They inched closer towards one another. There were damn near nose to nose before Tez stepped in between them.

"Come on now! Ya'll know we not about to do none of that up in here! Chill out! We around each other too much to be falling out over words! Fuck that shit! We need to be getting along! Save that beef shit for the streets! We family up in here! Feel me?"

"Nah Tez man. This nigga right here always calling men out their names! Ain't no hoes in here! You save that talk for them bitches! Then you talking about niggas ain't got no bread!

Nigga, I keeps me a bankroll!" Jay said flashing a messy knot of street currency.

"Ain't nobody impressed with that lil cash dude! You a lil nigga with lil paper if you ask me! You need to put that lil shit up! Like you say, ain't no hoes here! You better get your weight up lil homie! Brush up on your Call of Duty and dice game while you at it! That's what you need to be doing instead of talking shit to me!"

Bee pushed Jay in the chest. That caused him to stagger backwards. Jay was reaching for his strap. Tez immediately got up on him to grab his hand.

"Come on now nigga! You know better than that! You not about to pull shit on nobody! Chill dawg! You too fucking hot headed! You got to use your head instead of this piece. Niggas gone say whatever! You not about to let him pull you off your square are you?" Tez reasoned with the lil homie.

Jay focused on the words that were intended to calm him down. He needed to think a minute before blowing up. He took a long pull off his blunt.

"You know what? My bitch on her way to get me. I'm about to have a good day. I'm not about to let you fuck up my flow. You really need to watch who you talk crazy to man. We all know you around here. We know you like to talk shit; but we men before anything," Jay declared.

A car pulled into the driveway honking the horn. They moved to the window and saw a dark colored Mazda 929 with Jay's girl behind the wheel.

"Yo lil broad here fool. You have a nice one dude. Tell her to stay pretty," Bee laughed.

"Yeah ok. Watch your mouth. I'm out of here."

"Alright man. Take it light my dude. Be easy bro," Tez said.

Tez shut the door behind Jay. They watched the car pull away from the house. They locked the door and began to clean the mess left behind. All of the trash was gathered and placed in a large garbage bag. Tez washed his hands in the sink before drying them off on a paper towel. Bee stood against the wall in the kitchen.

"I don't know why you stay taking up for them old fag in the bag niggas! You know them niggas some hoes! Sweet ass mufuckas!"

"Why do you take it upon yourself to call people out? It's not your job to point shit out. Niggas got enough to worry about already. You be tripping for real."

"You act like you have to be the peace maker. What you gotta save everybody for? You must be feeling that lil dude. Is that it?" Bee questioned.

"You sound silly than a mufucka! You the one stay on his back! I don't say shit until you start making people feel uncomfortable. Don't nobody want to hear all that shit! You need to chill out for real!"

Bee moved closer into Tez's personal space. He stayed on his bully shit at all times. Tez was not one to back down though.

"I bet that lil nigga sweet as candy! What you got to say about that fool? I bet he go if I put a press on him! I know he soft as melted butter on hot popcorn! I bet you that! I be watching how he move! That nigga funny I tell you!"

"Dawg you worried about the wrong shit! Why you so concerned with another man's sexuality? That jail shit got you all fucked up!"

"I'll check myself alright! That lil nigga going for sure! I'm already knowing! You'll see!"

Tez just shook his head at Bee's obsession with the lil homie. There was no talking to him. His mind was made up. They continued to catch plays while sitting in the trap. They drank and smoked the evening away while playing the video game.

"I thought you was getting with your girl tonight?" Bee asked.

"What you talking about? I'm getting my bread and fucking with this game. We gambling or what?"

"Oh it's like that huh? You stay on that high powered bull shit! Yeah we gambling! I'm about to beat your ass on this game!" Bee laughed.

"I'm feeling no pain right now. This weed and liquor got me nice as hell. I'm still fucking you up in this game though!"

They each had a fifth of Remy Martin VSOP. They drank that shit right out the bottle. Tez's cell phone blew up the whole time they were sitting there. He would check it to send out a text periodically. Bee side eyed him the whole time.

"I see somebody popular. I never knew you were a celebrity man! I want to be just like you whenever I grow up! You da man!" Bee said in a sarcastic tone.

Tez was too buzzed to pay attention to the hater that Bee continuously proved to be.

"Nah man I'm just moving how I move. I put nothing above my paper. Them bitches can wait. I ain't got time for no nagging ass bitch on my back! I tell them hoes to move around!"

"I feel you homeboy. I used to chase my tail out in them streets. I wasted money, time, and everything else fucking with them cum buckets! You got the right idea for real. They on you heavy as long as you producing. When you stop, they up and out on you in a flash. I ain't never tripping though."

"Yeah I hear you. You done seen some shit ain't you? You be on a whole other tip man," Tez said.

"What you know dawg? You don't know me for real."

"I ain't about to speak on nobody else bullshit. I got plenty of my own trust me."

"Tez you just don't get it do you?"

"Get what? What's there to get? I see what it is for real. We don't have to speak on the obvious. We both know what it is."

"Well why don't you tell me what it is then Tez? Tell me about me please sir. Will you please?"

Bee stared at him. Tez took a deep breath for a moment before he conjured up the words for his associate. They were the only ones left in the trap so he let him have it.

"I see how you look at the young homie for starters. I definitely hear how you talk about him. You keep calling him a fag ass nigga. I really don't understand why his sexuality concerns you so much. You go in on him for no reason at all. He don't be bothering nobody."

"So what you saying? Can you spit it out since you obviously got me pegged already? Sounds like you watching me! Why you paying me so much attention?" Bee said in a raised voice.

"I'm saying you got a thing for the young boy! That's all I can see with the situation. Ain't nobody worried about who another nigga fucking unless he wants to fuck him! Now tell me if I'm lying on you! Tell me that you don't want to fuck the lil homie!"

"Mufucka!" Bee yelled grabbing for Tez's throat.

"Nigga!" Tez said reacting to Bee.

They locked up and tussled like two wild animals. Bee had Tez by his collar trying to lift him off his feet. Tez struggled to keep his footing as they danced around the kitchen. Tez had him tight around the waist and wasn't about to let go any time soon. Bee ripped Tez's shirt during the physical altercation.

"Aw man! You done tripped now mufucka! You done fucked up for real nigga! Come on with it! What you got? You ain't on shit!"

They moved all the furniture in the small room. Heavy breathing could be heard from them both. Tez ended up caking the shit out of Bee on the dingy floor. He then positioned himself on top of him for the pin move. They ended up nose to nose panting on one another.

"Get off me! You ain't on shit! Get your sweet ass off me! I know you ain't trying to grind on me nigga! I ain't no bitch ass nigga! Get the fuck off me! I ain't about to tell you no more!" Bee threatened.

"You ain't gone tell me shit! Nigga if you want up, get your ass up! You a lot of talk! Shut the fuck up! Say please or uncle and I might think about letting you up! If you can't do that, your ass will stay on your back!"

"I'm telling you! You gone make me fuck your bitch ass up! I know you don't want that for real! Is that what you looking for?"

They were having a full blown argument on top of one another. The scenario didn't look appropriate at all. To make matters worse, niggas' peters were starting to stiffen up.

"Nigga I know you ain't on hard? What the fuck is your problem? Let me up bitch!"

"That attitude right there is the main reason you got caked in the first place! It's also gone keep you there bitch!" Tez spit his own venom.

"Who you calling a bitch you old sweet cake ass boy? Now you done fucked up!"

Bee struggled to get from under Tez with no luck. He tried for a few seconds more before giving up. He laid his head back on the floor and stared at the ceiling. Tez laughed at the so called tough guy who was stuck on the floor. He got back in Bee's face to get the full effect of his frustration.

"Now who the bitch? I still ain't heard the magic words either!"

"You ain't gone hear them either! Fuck you! Sweet ass bitch nigga!"

"I got your sweet ass bitch nigga right here too!"

Tez grinded his hard cock into Bee's crotch which was rock also. Shit was definitely on the verge of going off the normal grid of things. Tez kissed Bee on his lips and waited on his reaction.

"Damn! You even kiss like a bitch! Come here!"

Bee grabbed Tez by his face to kiss his open mouth. Tez obliged and returned the favor. They made out on the floor as their breathing got heavier. Their hard dicks pressed up against each other. Bee began to remove Tez's shirt as the action slowly escalated. Tez rose up to pull Bee's shirt off. He kissed his chest and moved down to his pants. He undid them and pulled them off as well. Tez laughed to himself when he saw Bee in his bikini drawers. He pulled his sweats off before getting back on top of Bee. They tongue wrestled for a few more minutes until Bee flipped Tez over and snatched his boxers off. He smacked his ass as he pulled him up on his knees. Tez spread his cheeks and Bee stuck his head clean up his ass. He tongued his asshole and licked his nut sack all at once. That in itself pushed Tez into his zone.

"Goddamn that shit feels good! You know how to work that tongue huh?" Tez sighed.

Bee couldn't talk with a mouth chugged with ass and balls. He continued to work his number and Tez enjoyed every minute. Bee massaged his dick and bent it backwards in order to sample Tez's tool. He licked on his swollen dick tip to tease him a little. He then nibbled on it and Tez went bananas.

"Damn! What the fuck nigga? You sucking this dick from the back? You showing the fuck out now!"

Bee sucked and slurped minus the words. He let his mouth do all the talking. Tez had no idea what he had stepped into. He stuck his ass out so Bee could have more access to his goodie bag. Bee rotated between his asshole and hard cock. Tez was face down on the dirty floor trapped in ecstasy. Bee had him right where he wanted him. He took a finger and put it in his mouth to lubricate it. He then slid it up Tez's ass.

"I like that dawg! That's that shit right there!"

Bee smirked at his reaction. It only made his dick harder hearing those words. By now, his tongue and finger were in the same hole. He moved back down to the dick and took it in his mouth without even touching it. He finger banged Tez while sucking him off. Tez didn't really know how to act. He had never been worked in this manner before. He closed his eyes and let the moment overtake him. The scene playing out in the trap house was pure insanity. Bee wound his tongue around his shaft and balls. Tez's dick grew harder the more Bee's mouth danced up and down his ass.

"Suck my dick! Fuck yeah! Keep doing what you doing!"

Bee took the whole cock down his throat and began to make those gurgling noises. The spit soon drenched Tez's balls. Tez had to clench his fists because the shit was feeling too good. He opened his eyes and closed them repeatedly. He ended up losing his balance and falling on his side. Bee never let go of his dick. Tez lifted his leg in the air in a V-formation. Bee tongue fucked his ass while he massaged Tez's shaft that still glistened with saliva. He licked it from base to tip with careful precision. He tried his best to make eye contact, but Tez was acting shy.

"You scared to face me while I work this dick nigga? You shame or something? You was talking so much shit just a minute ago! Niggas be killing me!" Bee teased Tez.

Tez gritted his teeth while Bee licked and sucked on his dick head. Bee laughed to himself at the faces Tez displayed. He began to lightly munch on his nuts like they were cashews. He kept his hands on his prick moving them up and down. He sped up the motion and he noticed that Tez's body was starting to stiffen up just like his cock had already done. That meant that he was about to blow his load. Bee worked faster and the pay off came as expected.

"Awww! Aaahhh! Fuuuuucckkkk! Oh shit! Nigga! I'm about to buuuuust!" Tez announced.

Bee smiled as Tez squirmed on the floor. He sucked him until his balls were empty. Bee spit all that nut back onto Tez's stomach.

"Damn nigga! You spit all on me and shit! You a dirty mufucka for that one dude!"

"What the fuck you mean? You nutted didn't you? What the fuck is your problem? You thought I was gone keep that shit? That's your shit right there so you fucking keep it! I did what I was supposed to do! My job done! You better take your ass on in the bathroom and clean yourself off!" Bee laughed.

Tez got up. His knees were a tad bit weak from the load he just dispensed in Bee's mouth. He stretched and yawned for a minute. He turned to walk off as Bee smacked him firmly on his ass.

"What is up with you dude? That shit hurt like hell! Heavy handed mufucka!" Tez complained.

"Go head on with that soft ass bullshit! You sound like one of these girls out here!" Bee yelled.

Bee went to the ice box for a drink. He chose a beer after realizing there were no other choices. More traffic came to the door as more dollars were clocked at the trap house. Tez walked into the room where Bee sat.

"You drinking without me? That's how you doing it? You a wild mufucka Bee!" Tez complained.

"Put your mufucking clothes on! You up in this bitch half naked and shit! Get yourself together!"

Tez looked at him with his mouth wide open. He couldn't believe what his ears were hearing.

"What are you on dude? You know what's up! We in the middle of something here. At least we were! Now you on some other shit as soon as I step back in the room? We must be done here. Is that what you trying to say you fucking asshole you?"

"Who the fuck you raising your tone with nigga? You must've forgot what my name is!"

Bee stood and got in Tez's face. Nose to nose they were again. Tez was pissed and Bee found humor in that.

"Yo mufucking ass is fucked up! You gone in the head for real! You just sucked me off and now you acting all brand new! What the fuck are you on dude?"

With those words, they locked up again. They wrestled all over the room in a rather intense manner. Tez had his way with Bee. It was difficult for Bee to grab hold to Tez being half dressed and all. Tez flopped Bee around the room like it was nothing.

"Yeah mufucka! Talk your shit now!" Tez boasted.

Bee said nothing as he tried to grapple with this fired up young man. Tez stepped on a beer bottle and lost his footing soon after. He fell on his side and Bee took full advantage. He forced Tez on his stomach. Now Bee was in the cat bird seat.

"All that shit you talking! Look at you now! What you doing on your stomach? I can't hear nothing tough guy! You real quiet right now! I don't hear no tough shit now! You need to learn some fucking respect nigga! I'm about to teach you now!"

Bee snatched Tez's pants down to expose his bare ass. Tez acted as if he was trying to get up but he really didn't put up much of a fight. Bee slid his shit down and prepared to enter Tez's musty asshole.

"Damn nigga! You dry as a bone ain't you? Let me get you together right quick."

Bee spit in his hand and smeared his saliva all over his hard dick. He spit some more until it was covered in mucus. He stuck a finger in Tez's ass and rotated it a little. He slid it in and out before he placed yet another digit in his ass.

"Get your fucking fingers out my ass nigga! What the fuck is wrong with you? Let me up! Get up off me man!" Tez screamed while still on his stomach.

"Shut up! Don't you see me working back here? You fucking up my concentration dude!"

Bee jacked his dick in between Tez's butt crack. He also fingered him some more in order to loosen him up. After the finger came the dick. He pressed his dick head against Tez's anus and moved forward slowly. Tez felt the pressure and protested a little more.

"Man! What the fuck? Aaah!"

"Shut the fuck up lil nigga! You know you want this shit! Stop fucking playing with me! Shut up!" Bee shouted while holding Tez in place for the plowing.

Bee pushed his cock tip half way in his rectum. He took his time and continued to press on. Amidst the screams, his dick head managed to disappear. Bee felt the tightness of it and grew even harder. That only helped stretch the anal space more. Bee's forearm rested against the back of Tez's neck. He masterfully used his other hand to guide his black stick into the black hole. He laid flat on Tez. He spoke softly into his ear, "You liking that? This ass tight too! I see somebody been holding out! Mmmm! Damn!"

"Get the hell off me! Get the fuck off me man!" Tez said as he fake struggled.

A quarter of cock had now entered his asshole. Tears formed and fell from Tez's eyes. The situation had spiraled out of control. He was now trapped in a mean vortex.

"How that dick feel to you? You like this shit don't you? I don't hear nothing but breathing now! What's up with you now?" Bee said licking and nibbling on Tez's ear.

The flicking of the tongue on the ear was as sickening as the stiff cock he had in between his ass cheeks. The two men on the floor fucking was a sight the trap house had never seen. Bee slow grinded on Tez like he was listening to a smooth slow jam. His ass opened up as Bee crammed additional dick in it. Bee stuck his tongue too far in his ear and he tasted a nice load of ear wax.

"Ugh! Fuck nigga! When the last time you ran a q-tip through your mufucking ears! Your ear full of fucking wax! Ugh!" Bee said as he spat on the floor.

Tez didn't respond to Bee. How could he with the position he was in? The last thing he was worried about was his ears! All he could muster was grunts and groans. The weight of the man on top of him was taking a lot out of him. Every thrust took the wind out of him and also brought Bee closer to the orgasm he was seeking.

"Hmmm! Nigga this ass good! You like how I'm giving it to your ass? Huh? Mmm! Shit tight like a mufucka! You been sitting on this bitch huh?"

Bee got in the push up position and bore down on the ass up under him. Tez squirmed a little, but he wasn't trying to get away. He looked back at Bee and started to throw his ass back on him. Bee threw his head back as he applied more pressure behind his pelvic pumps.

"Mmm! Yeah! Throw that tight ass back on this dick! Oh yeah! That's my shit right there! You trying to work this nut on out of me ain't you? Keep that shit up and you gone make me squeeze one off in your ass! That's what you trying to do?"

"Yeah that's what I'm trying to do! You fucking the shit out me! That dick all in my ass! I want you to nut already! Damn! This is feeling weird but good all at the same time!" Tez chimed in.

Tez kept on throwing it back onto Bee. His arms flexed with every movement of his pelvis. He eased his penis out halfway before ramming it back in. That forced noise from Tez that Bee used for motivation.

"Shit! You pounding my ass like I owe you something!"

"You do owe me something!"

"What I owe you? Huh? Tell me what I owe you?"

Bee pumped his ass with more force. His ass slapped against Bee's pelvic area loudly.

"Mmmm! What you owe me? You owe me this nut that's on its way! That's what the fuck you owe me! You hear me? Huh?"

"Hmmm! Yeah I got it nigga! I'm getting it as we speak! I'm getting it good too! Mmmmm!"

Bee increased his speed as his orgasm approached. He showed Tez's ass no pity.

"I'm about to nut lil bitch! You hear me? This mufucka about to bust! Where you want me to shoot this shit at? I'm fixing to let it loose!" Bee announced.

"Mmmm! I don't care what you do! Just keep that dick running in and out my ass! Goddamn!"

He braced hisself as the activity in his ass intensified. Bee was now rabbit fucking Tez. They both were caught up in the moment. Bee nibbled on Tez's neck as the cream came.

"Uggghhh! What the fuck! I'm cumming right mufucking now! This nut going right in your shitter lil nigga! You feel that hot shit up your ass? You getting all this here!" Bee said deflating on top of Tez.

Tez shut his eyes and bit his lips in sheer delight. The sensation of what just transpired had him gone. He laid flat on the floor as Bee rolled off him and rested next to him.

He exhaled loudly, "Damn! I know my baby mama been trying to get in touch with me! She probably done hit my line a million times! Let me check my phone right quick! Damn!" Tez said.

"Your baby mama still around? I thought you been shook her off your tail. You must still be dipping in her cookie jar? That's what you on nigga? Playing both sides of the fence I see!" Bee laughed.

"So your baby mama knows how you out here moving? She know that you getting down with the get down? Huh? You all the way out there with it huh? Quit acting like people know the deal with you! You shoot your big ass mouth off, but you don't want people to know! Am I lying on you?" Tez tore into Bee something terrible.

The dumb ass grin on Bee's face vanished with that last drop of truth Tez dropped on him. He began to think as Tez took a hoe bath in the sink. The more he thought, the madder he became. Tez had touched on some sensitive nerves deep within Bee. His jaw tightened as he squinted his eyes through his anger. Tez meanwhile was in the bathroom cleaning his self up. Bee got up and walked down the hallway quietly. Tez never heard him until it was too late. Bee snuck up behind him and caught him with his pants down literally. Bee grabbed him around his neck and covered his mouth. Tez's eyes widened at the position he found himself in yet again. No screaming could be heard with Bee's dirty hand over his mouth. They both stood with their reflections staring back at them in the mirror.

"What's all that shit you was talking? Ain't nobody business who I stick my dick in! You hear me? I'm gone make sure you feel me on this one!" Bee warned.

He forced Tez down onto the sink. The dirty water was still in the sink. His face was now inches away from his own filth. Bee proceeded to guide his man missile right back in between Tez's ass crack. More spit was applied to his shaft as well as Tez's asshole. Bee jabbed a finger in his crevice for good measure. He kicked the inside of Tez's feet in order to spread his legs more. Bee let a nice string of spit fall onto Tez's ass.

"That ass still tight like I ain't even touched it! Damn! You like my snake in and out your ass nigga? Huh? Don't get quiet on me now! You weren't this quiet a few minutes ago!"

Tez didn't say a word. Guess you can't say much with a hand blocking your mouth. Bee started to get more into it as he loosened the grip on Tez's neck. His hands were now pulling Tez's ass apart. Every now and again, he would look in the mirror at Bee who was hard at work behind him. Bee was making faces and breathing strictly through his puffed jaws.

"Yeah! That's that shit I'm talking about! This our mufucking business right here! I don't fuck and tell! What about you nigga? You gone run your mufucking mouth?" Bee taunted.

Tez just looked at him before placing his head back on the sink. Water splashed onto the floor. The side of Tez's face was now wet. He continued to mute his reaction. He refused to feed Bee's monster ego any further. He could hear his phone ringing in the front room. In his mind, he wondered who that was on his line. His quiet behavior only made Bee fuck him faster and harder. He rammed Tez to the point that his head was trapped under the faucet.

"Mmmm! Yeah lil nigga! You taking this dick huh?" Bee said.

Still there were no words from Tez. He held his ground the best he could considering he had a hard cock in his anal region. His ass slapping against Bee was the soundtrack during their sexual tryst. Bee spread his ass cheeks as the drilling ensued. Tez had marks from the faucet on his face. Bee tried to wipe the marks away in a failed attempt with his hands.

"Awww! Look at the baby's face! Is your face alright dawg? Hmmm? I don't want you hurting yourself down there! I'm enjoying myself to the max back here though!"

Bee bent down to kiss Tez's face. He turned his head to slight Bee. Bee felt the sting of Tez's attitude firsthand. He kept on trying to kiss him anyway.

"You got an attitude? What's up with that? Come on now! Don't be like that!" Bee begged playfully into Tez's muted ears.

The silent treatment made Bee go that much harder. Tez said no words, but his breathing told the story. Bee looked at his reflection in the mirror. He smirked at the way Tez was all up under the faucet. Bee rubbed his neck in an effort to calm him down.

"This ass got me charged up something serious! You don't know what you got on you lil dude! You can ignore me all you want too! This here our business and its lovely from where I'm standing!"

Bee poked his ass with his meat with a rapid fire precision. The faces he made as the peak neared were ungodly. Tez just kept his head down and took all that Bee was dishing out to him.

"You lil bitch you! You about to make me bust again! That's gone be twice! Feel me? You just taking all this good dick ain't you? Huh? You not gone say shit? You just gone let me have all the fun by my goddamn self?"

Tez ignored Bee to the fullest. He heard every word because Bee was deep in his ear. The moment of the hour was well on its way and Bee had to let it be known.

"This dick about to blow on your ass nigga! You ready for the splash? Still no words for your boy? Huh nigga?" Bee said.

Finally, his love juice was unleashed. He let it off right in Tez's ass. Bee's dick emptied and his tough talk dissipated.

"Aaah! Mmmm! Fuck man! That was a good one there! This asshole only gets better with each fuck! Damn! Shit fire if you ask me!"

Bee loosened his hold on Tez in order for him to get up from the basin. He looked in the mirror at Bee who was standing there looking tapped out. The semen that was just deposited in him was now running down his leg.

Bee saw that and laughed at him, "Damn nigga! You look like you leaking for real! Guess you done blew a gasket or some shit! You better check yourself!"

"You stay talking some shit! That's all you do! Do you have anything of importance to offer? If not, please shut the fuck up! Would you please? Tez said washing his ass for the second time.

Bee pushed him into the sink and more water splashed onto the floor. Bee laughed and Tez shook his head. Bee left the bathroom and went into the living area. He put his shit back on and started playing the video game. Tez paid attention to the fact that Bee never got a wash cloth to clean himself.

"Nasty ass! Niggas be killing me! Talking all noise about the wrong shit!" Tez said to himself.

He made a mental note of that. Not only was Bee a loud mouth, but he was also a trifling mufucka. Tez walked into the room and tried to hug Bee from behind. Bee moved out of his reach.

"What the fuck is up with you dude? You on some old weirdo shit or something?"

"Huh? Weirdo shit? What the fuck is that shit? I'm just trying to show you a little love. Why do you insist on fucking up a good moment? Damn!"

"Nigga please! What good moment? I'm sitting here playing this game! I'm not bothering nobody! You come up behind me trying to hug on me like I'm your bitch! Don't do that shit to me! I ain't with all that nonsense! Good move, wrong dude though! I need to holla at my lil bitch! I want some pussy now!"

"Yeah I hear you alright. I can't figure you out at all man. You definitely a different breed if you want my opinion. Kind of fucked up if you ask me dude. You on a whole other tip for real," Tez said in a disgusted manner.

He left the ass cleaning cloth on the sink. He checked his phone to see several missed call/texts from his baby mama, Trina. He called her after reading the last message.

"Hello? What's up with you?" Tez said.

"Shit. What's up with your ass? I see you don't know how to answer! Hmmm?" She said.

"Don't start that shit now. I been gambling in the trap and you know how loud niggas get once money on the table. I ain't trying to go down that road with you."

"Ain't nobody tripping. I'm just letting you know how foul you are for being out all night. You should be spending time with your family. We need you home with us. I hope you got some money left because we're hungry."

"Yeah I hear you boss. I'm gone see what I can scrape up. It's hard times these days. You know I can't catch a fucking break out here. Just bear with me," Tez laughed.

"I'm bearing with you alright. You can't tell that I'm trying to have patience with your ass? You keep trying me like I don't have no feelings or something. Bring your ass home! I want some dick! Now come the hell on before I lose it!"

Trina ended the call with that. Tez sat for a minute to let her words sink in. Bee was still focused on his game. He wasn't paying Tez no never mind at all.

"What up man? Your lil bitch chewing your ass? You already done got a good screwing! Might as well go to the crib.

Your work done here. Your lady misses you. Don't make her wait on you. Them babies need you man. It's all good. I'll hold it down till you get back. You not gone miss shit."

"Alright man. I can tell when I'm no longer needed. It's cool dawg. I'm about to bounce on out of here. Come here and show me some love," Tez said.

He held his arms out for a hug. Bee gave him the strangest gaze ever. His face got all balled out of shape also. He could not believe what he was now hearing with his very own ears.

"What kind of gay ass shit are you on? You are a fucking sweet ass fruitcake nigga! You want some love? You need to take your sweet ass home to your family if you want love so bad!" Bee chuckled.

"You just gone be like this huh? You just gone fuck me and play dumb? Wow! Mufuckas kill me!"

Bee paid him zero mind as Tez bitched and moaned. Bee went through his phone as Tez got ready to leave. Tez tried to hug him once again to no avail.

"Man if you don't get your ass outta here! Why are you violating my personal space? You out of order for that one!"

"How am I outta order? What? I can't show you no love? You don't like that? Huh?"

"No I don't! Keep your mufucking hands to yourself dude! Your sweet ass tripping like a fool! You need to cut that shit out! You funny as fuck! You acting like we in a relationship!"

"Nah I ain't acting like we together. I was just showing love bro. I won't violate your personal space anymore. You won't have to worry about that. It's good. Can you please answer one question for me please?"

"What is that nigga? What kind of question you got for me?"

"Well since I can't hug you or violate your personal space, why is it that you can violate mines? You stuck your dick up my ass twice! That would be considered my personal space. Would you agree? I am listening bro."

Bee gave him a mean ass look for several minutes. Tez braced himself for whatever was about to come out of Bee's mouth. Bee didn't disappoint him one bit. He got in Tez's face so he could feel the seriousness of the matter.

"Let me answer your question nigga! Me sticking cock up your ass has nothing to do with personal space! Your sweet ass offered up some ass and you got what you got! That has nothing to do with me! That's all on your sweet ass! You hear me? Now back to me. I don't hug on no nigga! That ain't what I do! My personal space is just that! Don't hug me or try to do none of that punk shit! I ain't with none of that bullshit!" Bee said while pointing his finger in Tez's chest for confirmation.

Tez just stared at Bee after hearing his comments. Bee stared back at him without even blinking. No words were spoken for awhile as the men engaged in their childish stare off. Tez began to shake his head while rolling his eyes.

"Man you sound crazy as that one thang! How do you put hugging and fucking in the same category? That has my mind blown!"

"Man I don't give a fuck where your mind at! That shit ain't got nothing to do with me! Fuck your feelings you fruit loop ass mufucka! You trying to turn this here into some other shit! It ain't that serious dawg. It is what it is. Whatever happens in the trap stays in the mufucking trap! Now I can't tell a grown man how to act, but goddamn! Leave well enough alone and let this shit be over with! At least until next time!" Bee said with a wink.

Tez caught that shit instantly. He wasted no time in his response.

"Oh? Next time?" Tez asked with a raised eyebrow.

"I ain't about to go back and forth with you. It's cool dawg. My bad. I feel where you're coming from. It's your world man. Let me get out of here. I'm on my way home to my baby mama after I make a few stops. Alright man," Tez said on his way out the back door of the trap.

"Yeah get on home to your old lady and get you some real pussy! You hear me?" Bee laughed as he shut and locked the door.

Bee got back to the game. He drank some more liquor before realizing the shit was damn near gone. He kept playing the game until he passed out on the couch. Tez went home and got in the shower immediately. He got out and dressed for bed in fresh boxers and a crispy wife beater.

"Damn nigga! You been gone all day ain't you? I been hitting your phone! I know you heard me calling! You keep that fucking shit in your mufucking hand!" Trina barked.

"Baby I ain't trying to hear your mouth right now. Here you go. Count this up for me. Please and thank you. I would appreciate that ma'am," Tez said smirking.

She took the money and began her task of sorting it all out. She separated the various denominations in several piles. Her count yielded over $2,500.00. She rubber banded the paper and put it in a safe place. Tez was lying in bed chilling like villain. He smirked at how the bread shut her the fuck up. Once she secured the paper, she began to pick at him.

"You sleepy or something? I know you ain't had me up all night waiting on you just so you can fall out on me? Tell me I'm just tripping! Oh my fucking god! You gots to be shitting me! Iam so horny! I been reading this good ass book by Royce Winston called, "I Thought It Was Me." All they doing in there is fucking and sucking! That shit got my panties on fire! You know how horny my ass be baby! I want some of that good dick! Don't make me beg you for it!"

On that note, Tez rolled over and did his best to convince her that he was dead tired. It didn't work because she still wanted dick.

"Oh hell naw! You just gone put your back to me like that? You get on my last nerve!"

She hovered over his turned head and got close as hell to his ear. She made sure that he heard her every word. She began to pick at him for the attention she craved. She played with his ear. She pushed the back of his head. She even kicked him in his ass hard enough to make him damn near fall out the bed. Tez caught himself before he hit the floor.

"What the hell is going on in that head of yours? You really tripping now! I damn near hit the deck girl! Your ass would've been in trouble had that happened! Keep your feet to yourself!"

Now she had his attention.

"You turned your back to me baby. I want to fuck! I want that dick! You should be fucking me right now! I ain't seen you all day! You come up in this bitch and get ready for bed like it's all good! You the one tripping! What the fuck you on Tez?"

"I ain't on shit man! I been hustling, drinking, and smoking all day! I was getting money off that video game too! I apologize for being tired! I'm a fucking man! I'm not no goddamn robot! It's only so much time in the day! Can I rest for a little while?"

She stared at him while rolling her eyes periodically. This was a horny young lady who was dead set on dick. You had two people in the same bed with two totally different agendas. Tez was determined not to fuck her no matter how much she protested.

"Yeah I hear you. You acting like you ain't never came up in this bitch drunk and high and ready to fuck something! Now tell me if I'm lying on your faking ass! You on some real bullshit right now mister! Let me find out you fucking with more than money and video games! You can think you slick all you want!"

"I'm not trying to hear none of that fuck shit! Gone head and talk your crazy shit! You sound stupid as fuck!"

"You need to quit playing and gimme that dick!"

She grabbed at his genitals before he rolled back over. Tez wasn't for any of that bullshit. He held his ground by damn near balling up into the fetal position.

"I know you not about to play me like this! Well fuck you then! One thing I'm not about to do is beg for some dick that supposed to be mines in the first place! Fuck you nigga! I know exactly what to do right now!"

Tez was all ears as she made her announcement. She started rambling through her night stand drawer. The search ended as soon as she found what she was looking for. A muffled buzz came out the blue. Tez rolled over to find her playing with her hairy pussy by way of dildo. Tez turned his nose up at her fuzzy ass bush.

"Damn! You ain't got no razors? That shit looking real fucked up!" Tez complained with a smile.

She gave him a look and continued to pleasure her damn self. He couldn't help but to pay her a little attention. It's kind of difficult to ignore a chick playing with her pussy in front of you. She had her legs open as she concentrated on her own clit.

"Mmmm! Mmmmm! Shhhh!"

Her moans sparked even more engrossment from her difficult man.

"Damn! You just gone do shit like that right here? You wild as hell! Fuck you! I'm taking my tired ass to sleep! Fuck you one more time too!" Tez said.

She had no words for him. She was looking for some action and Tez wasn't with it at all. He tried his best to go to sleep as the buzzing and moaning persisted.

"Oh yeah! Oh shit! Mmmm! Goddamn! Fuck yeah! I'm about to cum all over myself! Owww! Mmmm!"

Tez said nothing as her body jerked next to him. She put her toy away and turned off the light.

"It's a damn shame that I have to fuck myself with a whole nigga here with me. That's that bullshit, but whatever! Have a good night nigga!" Trina said with much attitude.

"Yeah whatever," Tez said without looking at her.

He had more on his mind than her pussy. His day had been nothing short of eye opening. He could still feel his asshole tingling from his earlier activity with Bee.

"I can't believe shit went the way it did. That nigga sure did toss me a curve ball. I can't wait to get back to the spot. It ain't about the money either," he thought to himself as he fell into a slumber.

The next day, he jumped out the bed ready to get in the wind. Trina slept away as he quietly got dressed and slid out the door. He made a bee line back to the trap house to see what Bee had running. He went around the back door and knocked for a few minutes. There was no answer. He found that as odd cause there was always someone there. Money was always falling through, so something was definitely off. He went from window to window to see if there was anyone home. He circled the entire house before he remembered the basement windows around back. He looked in the first one and saw absolutely nothing. He was feeling like his fake stalking was all for nothing. That is until he reached the last window. That one had exactly what he had come for. He had to rub the dust off the pane to see more clearly. His smile suddenly transformed right on his face. On the couch asshole naked were Bee and the young boy Jay he was picking on the other night. The young boy was on his knees giving Bee major skull. Bee's head was thrown back in pure delight. Upon seeing such a sight, Tez backed up from the window and house all together. He now realized that maybe it was not all about him. He realized that he wasn't anything special to Bee. He realized that Trina had a right to act the way she did a few hours ago. He realized that he had a bruised ego and tender ass from his dealings with Bee. With tears falling from his eyes, he dialed his baby mama to apologize and hopefully keep his home life intact. Even though he liked mustard on his hot dog, her sweet pussy would have to do. Maybe if he was lucky, she might allow him entry to her brown eye. That was his only option after being shit on by another man. He made his way home to seek comfort in a woman's arms that he rejected hours ago. Karma a funky hoe ain't she?

Chapter 3

Power Struggle

"I'm gone be late as hell trying to find this place!" I cursed out loud.

I was on my way to a job interview in the city. I flew down Choteau Ave. and swerved onto the Ameren/U.E. lot. I parked and ran into the lobby. There was a desk visible as soon as I emerged from the carousel doors. There was a female security guard posted. I asked her about the person that I was supposed to be seeing.

"Let me call him to let him know that you are here," she said smiling.

She hung up the phone and said, "You a cutie. I ain't never seen you up in here before. You trying to get you a gig here?"

"Yes ma'am."

She busted out laughing, "Boy! I'm old, but not ancient! You can call me Netta. You Terry right?"

Before I could ask her how she knew, I remembered that I told her before she made the call.

"Yes that's me. Nice meeting you Ms. Netta."

"There you go with that old crap. Just call me Netta. I see you have a problem with following simple instructions. I'm gone have to get on you about that!"

Shit was getting really weird at this point. I was waiting on my contact person, but I guess my interview had already begun unbeknownst to me. She was grinning and flashing them bedroom eyes at me. Her skin tone was caramel dipped. Her face was devoid of any makeup. Her deep dimples were on display whenever she spoke or smiled. Her teeth were small, white, and most importantly, straight! Netta was definitely a sight to behold.

The contact came to the desk and we walked to the elevator.

"Make sure you come by to see me once you done Terry. You hear me?"

"Yes ma'am," I said winking as the elevator doors shut.

I knew that pissed her off, but fuck it! I did it anyway! I went on up and handled my business as far as the interview was concerned. I shook hands with the overly tanned white gentleman and I was on my way back to the lobby. I turned my visitor badge in to Netta who was still smiling.

"Terry! What you up to for the rest of the day?"

"Shit for real. What's up?"

"It's getting close to lunch time. How about we head down to the Eat Rite diner?"

"Hmmm. That doesn't sound like a bad idea. Yeah, let's do that. You ready to go right now?"

Netta rose up from behind the desk and the male security guard sat in the chair. That is when I got a real gander at her body. She was no taller than 5'3''. Her boobs were big, but not stupid big. She was thick as fuck from the waist down. Her creased pants were holding on to all that ass for dear life. I then focused on her long black hair which didn't have a track in sight. I would have to investigate the authenticity of her mane a little later.

"Let me go to the bathroom before we go. Wait right here for me."

She excused herself and left me at the desk. For some reason, he was eyeing me pretty hard. I did the head nod at fool and he didn't return the gesture. Fuck 'em! I didn't need no new friends no way! I stood with my back to the hater for the rest of my time in the lobby. Netta came up from behind me and tickled my ear. I turned slightly and she was smirking at me. I looked over her shoulder and dude still had his mug stuck on mean.

"You ready to roll baby?" Netta asked.

"Yep."

"Come jump in with me. We don't need to take both cars. Are you cool with that baby?"

The vibes she gave off put me at ease. It's nothing like being around someone who constantly makes sure that you are taken care of.

"Yeah. That's alright with me."

We walked to her older model Cutlass Supreme and got in. She fiddled around with her keys as I looked around her car. There was shit everywhere. Clothes on the back seat, old fast food bags, and wrappers littered the floor. Blunt roaches filled the ashtray along with old chewing gum. From the looks of things you could assume that she didn't have a man. If she did, he was one lazy son of a bitch.

"You straight baby?" Netta said slapping my thighs.

That snapped me out of my trance I was in from seeing all the clutter.

"Yeah I'm cool," I lied.

"You getting pretty quiet on me over there. What's on your mind?"

If I told her how I was really feeling that would fuck up our flow. Now we couldn't have that! Her hand was still on my thigh. I looked down then over at her.

"I was just thinking how well my interview went. Dude seemed like he was digging what I had to say," I lied to her once again.

She didn't say another word. She let her hand do the talking for the rest of the ride. It slid gently up and down my leg. It was very soothing if you want to know the real deal. We made it to the spot and it was crowded as expected. Hell, it was lunch time. We were in luck because most of the patrons were ordering their food to go. We sat at a table and had some small talk before placing our orders.

"So how old is your lil tender ass? I can smell the milk on you from here," she laughed.

"I'm 21," I said with a straight face.

She was beginning to get on my nerves with how she carried me like a baby. I had to keep my cool cause I really didn't know what direction this situation was headed in.

"Mmmmm! You are legal huh baby? Fresh meat! I love me some fresh meat! That dick get hard and stay hard for no reason! Goddamn! I done struck me some good old ghetto gold!"

"What's ghetto gold? If you don't mind me asking."

"Look down for me," she instructed.

That request threw me, but not enough to honor it. I did exactly what she told me to do. By then, the waitress had come to take out orders. Netta got some chicken and I got a burger. I sipped on some water while the food was being prepared.

"What did you see when you looked down Terry?"

"I saw my lap."

"What's in your lap? You might need to check again just to make sure."

"I got a napkin in my lap."

"Right, but what's under my, I mean your napkin? My bad. I'm a little hot and bothered over here. Don't mind me at all. It's been awhile for me."

"Been awhile for what?" I asked already knowing.

"Since I had some dick! My old man took his dumb ass to the military. He left me here by myself. He does look out for me money wise; but sexually I'm about to explode! I'm tired of playing with this good pussy all by myself. Shit done got old. Phone sex with my old man only makes me want to get the real thing. You follow what I'm saying?"

"Damn, that's fucked up for real. Sorry to hear that."

I never lost eye contact with her. She was now licking her full lips. They had a nice sheen to them. My mind was all over the place while sitting there. My cock was damn near touching the bottom of the table through my trousers. For some reason, at that very moment, Netta peeked under the table. The napkin appeared to be floating now. She looked back at me and licked her lips once more.

"That dick hard ain't it? It's about to bust right out them pants! Ain't it? Mmmm!"

From her reactions, I could tell that she was a real dick freak. Even though they are out here in abundance, you don't run into them on a regular basis. Looks like I done discovered a lil gold my damn self!

"You looking at it ain't you? You know what this situation is over here. Quit acting slow!"

I got fake tough with her and a big smile covered her face.

"Whoo! Mouth watering and getting all dry at the same time! See what you doing to me?"

"I ain't done nothing but sit here. Now the fact that you got my dick about to flip the table is a whole other story!"

We laughed as our food was being brought to the table. We dug in as the discussion matured.

"So Terry. What's your relationship status at the present? You married? Baby mama? Living with someone? How many bitches you fucking? I know you got plenty of bitches around here. What's up? Let me know if I'm wrong or not!"

I don't appreciate when someone automatically draws a conclusion about you and whatever type of situation you may or may not have going on. That shit is wack for real! I did my best to hold in my disdain towards her comments.

"Well, you know what they say about people who are always assuming? But anyway, let me get to your question. I do have a girlfriend. No I don't have any kids. We are thinking about getting a place together, but nothing yet. I hope you are satisfied with my responses."

I took another bite of my cheeseburger with everything on it. I chewed and waited on her to shoot something back across the table at me. There was silence while we enjoyed our chosen dishes.

Netta wiped her mouth before continuing, "So is she the only bitch you fucking? You forgot to answer that one. I can wait."

I smiled, "I get a little pussy here and there when the opportunity presents itself."

"Yeah, I done heard that one before! Something like yesterday to be exact! Is your girlfriend the jealous type? She know you be fucking other bitches? Does she fuck other niggas? Do you practice safe sex? Are you clean? The reason I asked is because my dude off in the military. I ain't supposed to be doing nothing while he gone. You feel me?"

I washed my food down while she attempted to shove more shit down my throat. I wasn't buying any of it, but I let her speak her peace.

"Yeah I hear you. Yes she is jealous. She does her thing and I do mines. We're kind of on the down slope of our relationship. The trust is gone between us. I practice safe sex at all times. I even wear rubbers when I get brain from chicks. I try to keep myself as clean as possible. Does your man know you are creeping around on him while he's protecting our country? You know you ain't shit for that one!"

I couldn't resist going in on her a little. I knew she probably didn't give a shit either way.

"I got that bitch ass nigga wrapped around this finger right here."

She held up her pinky for effect. She let me know that she had no respect for men right then and there. Here this man is risking life and limb and she over here trying to get some freak shit cracking!

"That nigga been open off this good shit for years! I make him beat his dick over the phone whenever we talk! He better keep his dick in his fucking fatigues! He knows better than to dip off in some strange pussy! Fuck him! Let's get back to your sexy ass! How big is your dick?"

I liked her style thus far. She said whatever came to her mind. It was definitely a turn on if I do say so myself.

"My dick is decent. I haven't had any complaints. I'm not porno size, but I'm far from pinky size also. It depends on the condition of your fuck box. If you got a lot of miles on that bitch, then we may have a problem."

"Miles? You talking about how much dick I done had between my legs? I had a baby in my teenage years. I was head over heels for his sorry ass. I was with him for a few years off and on. I ended up meeting my new dude during one of our breaks. I been fucking with him ever since. He gave me a ring along with a marriage proposal before he left. I took it, but I never wore it. I ain't married, so why should I act like it? Fuck that dumb shit! He gone have to do more than that if he wants to make an honest woman out of me!"

Here was another self entitled, unappreciative female. Imagine that.

"If you say so. How long has he been away on duty? Sounds like he putting in work. He did give you a ring. Most niggas gone give you a ring around your fucking eye instead of that finger!"

"If he even think about putting hands on me he better think again! Get his ass locked up quick, fast, and in a motherfucking hurry!"

We laughed at her last remark. I couldn't understand why she was going so hard on her future husband. Why accept his ring if he doesn't make you happy? Damn!

"You crazy. You know that already though. Decent convo so far. I'm glad I came here with you."

"I'm happy to have you here also. It's not every day that I am blessed to be in the presence of a handsome young man such as yourself. You have definitely made an old woman's day. I'm over here on fire thinking about what I want to do to your ass! My pussy been wet since I first laid eyes on you! Do you have any idea of what I want to do to you? My pussy soaking through my cotton panties! Damn boy!"

"Your ass crazy Netta."

"You got that right! I'm going crazy over you! It's all your fault! I have to have you! Fuck your lil fake ass girlfriend! You gone be my new boo! I gots to have you for my damn self! What side you stay on?"

"I'm from the East Side."

"You have a problem coming to see me? I stay in the Central West End area. That works out great for the both of us. You can have your lil bitch on your side and come over here and fuck around with me. Does that work for you Terry?"

"It sounds fine to me. I don't want to bump heads with nobody on your end. These niggas be crazy about they bitches these days. I don't need you to be putting me in no fucked up position. I don't want to die behind no pussy. Feel what I'm saying? Now is the time to speak up if you got somebody. If you trying to get somebody jealous, please don't do it with me. I know too many cats that met they maker over some funky ass box! I can't go like that! No sir!"

She had to feel my conviction at that moment. I was being way real with her whether she knew it or not.

"You have to know that I go to work and go home to my daughter. My man is overseas and I'm not messing with nobody. I mean, niggas be trying to get in my pants all the time. I ain't fucking with none of them. I just keep to myself. I don't have time for the games people play out here. No thank you. You can keep that shit to yourself. I'll pass. You don't have nothing to worry about if you come to my spot. It's my spot. I run that mufucka the way I please! You come over and my baby gone be in her room. She don't be in my business. I'm grown and I do whatever I want. I would not have you come into a dangerous situation. You safe with me. That's why I asked about your girlfriend. I don't want any problems with no one. I got too much to lose!"

I had no choice but to look at her sideways. The shit she was talking sounded like some bull I heard the other day. Chicks will tell you whatever they think you want to hear. There was a natural hate between St. Louis cats and East St. Louis cats. The Mississippi River separates us. If you jump across any bridge you can land on either side in less than three minutes. You fuck around and get caught out of bounds and it can mean life or death. I wish I was making this all up but I'm not.

"Yeah, I hear you. Cats be on some way out shit. I ain't about to go out on no sucker shit. I hope you are meaning all that you are saying to me. Shit can be risky if you're not careful. I want to leave nothing to chance. I'll be all the way over your spot by myself. I can hold my own, but a heads up is always good just in case there is a slight hint of danger. Do you feel what I'm saying?"

"I do and I understand everything that you are saying to me. It's just me and my baby at the house. I must protect her at all costs. She is my world. I love her to death. I would not invite danger to my doorstep. I work and she goes to junior high school. That's our routine of what we do. Nothing will be allowed to interrupt what we got going."

She seemed sincere, but a grain of salt was still taken with every word. I didn't trust her. I would definitely take the usual precautions before venturing into a foreign hood. I didn't give a shit what she was talking about!

We finished our plates as the check was dropped damn near in my lap. I reached in my pocket and she grabbed the check and paid for it. I made a mental note of her gesture.

"I invited you out remember? I will pay the bill. Do you want anything else?"

"I'm cool. Thank you."

We got up from the table and walked outside. She held the door for me to walk out. She was really pouring the shit on thick. I enjoyed the attention, but I still kept my eyes on her all the while.

"What you got up for the rest of the day? You gone fuck your lil girlfriend later on?"

"I am going to kick back by myself. I'm not fucking anyone later if that's fine by you."

"As a matter of fact, that's not alright with me."

"And why not?"

"Because I would like to fuck you later if you don't mind. Now is that alright with you?"

She just hijacked my entire thought process. Her response was totally out of left field.

"I'll have to check my schedule and see what's up. Let me get back to you."

I had to go ego on her just to let her know that there was no thirst dwelling within me.

"Are you fucking kidding me? You gone get back to me? That's an answer that I've never heard before!" She laughed.

She turned onto the Ameren/UE parking lot. I knew she had probably heard plenty of shit, but never that one. I had to laugh to myself for the point I just made. Score one for the good guy!

"Yeah! I'll holla back at you shortly. You got a jack that I can hit you on later?"

"You mean my number? Yes you can have my number. You can call me to let me know once the dick is ready for me. Hopefully my pussy doesn't get dry with all of the waiting on your important ass!"

We both had to laugh. She wrote her number down on an old Captain D's receipt that she got off the floor board. Before giving it to me, she grabbed a handful of my shit.

"I need some of this mufucka in my boring life! You gone give me some or not? Does your lil girlfriend suck your dick like you like it? If this was my dick, I would suck you dry on a regular basis!"

She hit the nail clean on the head as far as I was concerned. She was indeed speaking my language. I loved me some head and my fake ass girlfriend was not providing me with anything of the sort. My cock stayed in desert mode while dealing with my girlfriend. You never bad talk your mate to anyone; especially not to someone who is trying to take their spot. I was tempted to, but I held my tongue.

"That sounds good to me. We'll have to see what it is that you are speaking of. I have nothing much to say on that one. We'll see," I said rubbing my chin.

"I guess you one of them nonchalant niggas. You just so cool sitting there. Like what I'm saying ain't fazing you at all."

I just sat there while she massaged my manhood through my pants. Her thirst was evident. I did my best to conceal mines. It was pretty difficult with a stiffy brewing in my crotch. I held my own nevertheless.

"I'm just taking it light. Let me write my number down. I like what you are saying so far. You seem pretty cool."

I wrote my digits on an old Wendy's bag. There was trash scattered all over the car. Why not?

"So when is a good time to call you? I don't want no trouble from your lil girlfriend. You know my end open. I'm good. What about you?"

"I'm free between 2:30 pm and 12:30 am. That's when she takes her ass to work. I can play during those hours. She calls to check on me, but it's nothing."

"I hear you loud and clear. You will be hearing from me before you know it. I'm sure you get offers to fuck every day of the week. That's why you not tripping off me grabbing your hard dick. You make me want to pull it out and show you what I'm made of. I'll just save that for later. All you have to do is answer when I call you. Can you do that for me Terry?" She said licking her lips.

"We can save it for later. That works for me. I will look out for your call if and when you do call. I will not hold my breath for your information! Just so you will be aware. If you call, you call. If you don't, you don't. The choice is yours."

I got out the car on that note. I slammed her door without saying another word. It's always best to leave a bitch hanging with her mouth open. I got in my shit and left the lot. My girlfriend called to see what I was up to. I was in super high spirits. We were always having problems and today was no different. I cut the conversation short in order to maintain my current vibe. Anytime she felt like my mood was too chipper, she would do her best to crush my spirits. I went home and took a nice shower. I had a great day and it was only room for it to get better. I relaxed for a few hours until my phone began to ring.

"What up man? What you got going tonight? Let's go see some pussy at the Slip! What's up?" My homie Chris said.

"What up? You always want to see some damn pussy! Shit don't get old to you huh? Crazy ass dude!"

Chris was someone that I grew up with. He was a solid brother that I could tolerate from time to time. We had been going to strip clubs since we were teenagers. I'm a cheap ass dude who grew up on the notion that pussy was free. I didn't mind going to the shake joints, but I did mind paying to see them naked. I would go and sit at the bar and drink. Anyone knows that strip club etiquette is if you sit at the stage, your ass better be paying! I learned that the first time I stepped foot in a white titty bar in Brooklyn, IL. I paid to get in and made a bee line towards the stage. There were two white chicks on the stage doing their thing. The rock music was blasting "Pour Some Sugar On Me." The waitress asked me about my choice of drink for the day. I forgot to mention that it was broad daylight and probably no later than one o'clock in the afternoon. I wasn't sure what to order, so she suggested that I try the "Purple Hooter." She brought me a mini sample of the drink and it tasted decent. I focused on the dancers on the stage who were earning their pay for the day. One of them was tall, slender, and her boobs were blown up artificially. She had that wet, stringy ass hair with colored streaks in it. She had on a lingerie outfit that looked cheap as fuck. It was purple with matching tall heels. She danced to the music and moved closer to where I was seated. My drink arrived and I took a sip. I looked up and she was right in front of me. She flashed her fake tits and stuck her tongue out. I was unfazed. She took her top off to expose her bare chest. Her boobs never moved while she fake danced in my face. She squatted down while rotating her bony hips. I was still unfazed by her actions. You could see her pussy print through her g-string. She then jumped from the stage and into my lap. She grinded her narrow ass into me as she stared me square in my face. She whispered in my ear as I grabbed her ass with my free hand. A bouncer immediately came out of nowhere and tapped my shoulder.

"Uh excuse me sir," said the overgrown white dude in the tight suit.

"Yeah, what up?" I snapped back.

"I'm going to have to ask you to not touch the ladies sir. Please and thank you because the next time you will be escorted out of here."

I looked at the dude and back at her. I'm in a strip club for the first time and this happens? You can't touch the girls but you can pay to see them dance half naked? What kind of bullshit is that? She continued to rub her scrawny ass on me. She then climbed back on stage and pulled her g-string out away from her crotch area. I leaned in to get a gander at her freshly shaven snatch. I sat back in my seat and kept on drinking. She looked at me and gave me one of them sly grins with her head tilted to the side. I smiled back at her. After a few uncomfortable seconds, her smile disappeared.

"Now sugar, if you are going to sit here at the stage and watch, you must tip. When I pull my thong out for you, it's not just to look at my pretty pussy. It's also for you to place money in there. Is this your first time in a strip club? When the girl pulls her g-string out, that means you should drop a dollar in. You follow me so far?"

"Ok I follow you. I was not aware of that policy. Thank you for pointing that out to me. I have already been told that it was a no hands situation going on here."

"No problem sweetie. Happens to the best of us. You enjoying yourself thus far? My name is Cassie. How is that drink?"

"I'm Terry. My drink is fine. Nice meeting you. My bad, here you go," I said putting money in her panty cash drawer.

I sat back and let what was said to me sink in. I was totally unaware of the many rules pertaining to strip joints. I didn't like any of it. Every few moments she danced, here came the g-string being pulled out. I caught on real fast to what was going on. The waitress offered me another drink. I took the bait, but this round would be different. I got my ass up and moved to the bar. I made my mind up to never sit at the stage again. I would rather give the bartender my money if I had to choose. You couldn't lay a fingernail on the ladies anyhow. That began my disdain for supporting strippers. Chris, on the other hand, developed a pure love for the working girls shaking ass for a living. He was fond of this older one who had gold teeth, light skinned, and was taller than normal. She wore a bob style wig. How do I know it was a wig you may ask? Well, I happen to know a fucking wig when I see one! Her light colored eyes were chinky as fuck. Her gold teeth were on display whenever she smiled. He tipped her during her entire set. When she was done, she got off the stage and pulled Chris into the private area. That was even more money down the drain. We came with a couple hundred dollars in our pockets. I had no intentions of leaving with them empty either. Chris left out the private area looking like he had hearts in his eyes. We left and all he wanted to do was talk about his new stripper friend. I don't know what she said to him, but he actually believed that she was digging him. His pockets were indeed deflated. I don't care to know what goes on behind the dark curtain. I do know that if it's going to break you and leave you penniless, you can shove that bullshit in your fucking g-string!

"Man, I'm feeling like tricking off something serious! I done picked up rent money for a few of my properties today. I'm trying to go crazy on them hoes! You rolling or what?"

I did not have to think neither long nor hard on the question he posed to me.

"Nah Chris. I'm gone sit this one out. I'm gone lean on back and kick my feet up. You need to take that paper and put it up. Giving them hoes all your bread ain't cool at all. I'm not gone keep you from having a ball in there. Get someone to go with you though. Safety first and always."

"Alright man. I'll catch you some other time. I was gone treat for all the drinks. Whatever you wanted, I had you. You sure you not trying to fuck with it?"

"Be careful and kick it for me man. I have to get my mind right. Thinking cap, you know?"

"Yeah, maybe I'll fuck with you when I leave Brooklyn. Go get a bite to eat or some shit. Take it easy with your thinking cap on!"

We hung up and I just sat still for a minute or two. I was having a splendid day so far. I had a new job on the horizon, a new freak on deck waiting to go, and money in my pocket. I had every reason to treat myself, but I held back. I was thinking about getting me something to drink though. Maybe some cognac or tequila. I was in a dark mood for real. I jumped in the ride and went to Sam's for some liquor. I got there and headed to the spirits section. I had to stand there for a minute to take all my options in. I decided on some Courvoisier cognac and was out of there. I got home and threw that fifth in the freezer. I poured some water from a Voss bottle. I looked out the window and the day was still beautiful. I was feeling so good that I went and worked out in my back yard. I did pushups, jumping jacks, etc. The phone started ringing mid way through one of my many sets. I got up to answer it and a smirk inched across my face when I realized it was Netta.

"What up? How may I be of service?"

"Now I can appreciate that. How can you be of service to me you ask? Well, you can start by bringing me that dick! I got some plans for it! My mouth needs you ASAP! Every hole I got is begging to be stuffed! Can you please handle my request?"

"Why yes ma'am. I believe my department can fill your order. Just give me the lay out and we will go from there."

"The layout? What's that?"

"Where do you stay? How safe is the hood? Do you have dick covers? What you got to drink? Where are your stalkers? I need to know all that."

"Damn! You don't hold back do you? I live off Gibson Ave. My hood is pretty safe for the most part. I've never had any problems. I have plenty of condoms. All sizes too! I have zilch to drink on my end. You can bring something if you want. I'm a smoker, so you already know how that goes. I keep telling you that my fiancée is abroad. I ain't messing with nobody. You will be my first since he been gone. Anything else you need to know?"

"Hmmm. Sounds like you covered everything I asked. I appreciate your honesty. What makes me so lucky to receive your honey pot?"

"Damn baby. I been thinking about you all day. I been asking myself the same question. I don't know. It's just something about you Terry. You're sexy and I would like to know what your cum tastes like. I haven't had no good dick since before my dude left. He was not fucking me correctly at all. I need for you to help clean up his mess. Can you do that Terry?"

She threw the sex talk in there as sort of a distraction. Never did she put my nerves at ease about the threat level. I already knew to take matters into my own hands. I would take the necessary precautions to make sure I was protected my damn self!

"I can do that. I'm about to get dressed. What time are you talking about?"

"Let's get it popping around eight. I stay in the thirty five hundred block. You will see my car out front. It's a two family flat. I stay on the "B" side. You can park anywhere, but my street is a one way. You can call when you get on Manchester. I will talk with you until you get outside my door. I hope that makes you relax a little more. I want you at ease for the most part. I don't want you tense. I want you hard and fucking the shit out of all my holes! That's all I want. I want to fuck you Terry. Can you allow me to do so?"

"That's cool. We can get together. Let me get dressed and I'll be headed your way. I'll call once I dip off the highway. See you in a minute."

I took another shower. I put on baby lotion, baby powder, Vaseline, and a few slight sprays of Vince Camuto cologne. I threw on a short sleeve Ralph Lauren polo shirt with some cargo shorts and some Clarks walking shoes. I put a handful of rubbers and peppermints in my pockets. I put my baby .45 in my hidden waistline holster. I then placed the larger .45 into the console. You must be prepared for whatever may come your way. I didn't trust anything Netta had to say. I only trusted me and my gut. They both were telling me to go and plug her like a utility socket. I made a drink to go. I also put the rest of the bottle in the trunk. I flew down highway 64/40 west and exited on Kingshighway and made my way to Manchester. Netta lead me right to her front door as we talked on the phone. I parked and got the bottle out the trunk. I walked up the steps and into her door.

"Damn baby! You smell good enough to eat! Mmmm!" She said.

She rubbed her hands together as she walked me straight to her bedroom in the back of the house. The candles were burning and the mood was set in motion. I sat on the couch which was next to her bed. She sat next to me and her hand went right to my cock area. She touched the gun and her facial expression switched right up.

"Is this what I think it is?"

She took the pistol and put it next to me. She then undid my shorts. Netta took my meat out and stroked it gently.

"You are a nice size! Look at you! Shit hard as an Eskimo brick too!"

Netta got on her knees to bless with me some lip service. The t-shirt she wore rose up to show her blue thong underwear. I lifted up my arm so she could have more action at my man. I had my drink in one hand and her supple ass in the other. Before she put my dick in her mouth, she spit a large gob of mucus on the tip of my manhood. The spit slid down to my balls as she jacked me off. Her tongue danced around the head of my shaft. She kissed it before making the head disappear in her mouth. The sucking noises she made me get me that much harder.

"Mmmm! This dick tastes so fucking good! Let me get them balls! Can't forget them balls!"

Netta was proving to be my kind of girl indeed. Any woman who refuses to neglect your balls is alright with me! I mean, who wants a wet dick and desert balls? I used my middle finger as a probe to test the dampness of her thong. Her pussy was slowly making a puddle in the crotch area. I moved it to the side to massage her fat lips. She wiggled her ass to allow my finger to escape deeper into her soggy love hole. We were now fully engulfed in the moment.

"Mmmm! Put that finger in my ass Terry! I want you to play in my asshole!" Netta demanded in between licks and sucks on my dong.

She got back to spitting and jerking on my meat. I did exactly as she told me seconds earlier. I fingered her pussy for the last time before inserting it right into her dook shoot. The more I pushed it in, the wilder she got.

"Quit playing and finger bang this ass! Don't be scared of it! Put that finger all the way up in there! I love that shit!"

I would never hold up progress. I plunged my finger all the way in to the knuckle. Her ass gripped my digit rather snug. I rotated it while slowly moving it in and out. Her head game had me impressed thus far. She definitely took pride in her work. As the action grew more intense, Netta raised up to remove her thong and t-shirt. I stood up to remove my outer garments as well. She stayed sucking and pulling on me until I grabbed her hands. I took them off my cock so I could face fuck her more effectively. I don't really like chicks jacking me while they perform fellatio on me. I kind of look at it like they're cheating. Make me cum with your mouth! Fuck your hands! I got my own fucking hands! She sat back on the couch and I stood on it in order to bury my pole down her throat. My pubic hairs doubled as her mustache at the moment. As I pumped her face, I noticed that she was playing with her pussy with the same hands I just took off my dick. Her moans were muffled due to the amount of dick that had been freshly deposited in her throat. She then grabbed my hips and forced me to fuck her mouth even harder. I put my hands against the wall to maintain my balance while standing over her on the couch. She moved my hips with such force that I looked down to see if my shit hadn't poked out the back of her head. There were two thick white streams of saliva racing down each side of her busy mouth. The left stream of spit eventually made it down onto her chest. The right one soon followed. I was fucking her mouth like it was her pussy. I ran my finger across my nose to do a quick smell check. I at least expected an ass like smell, but I smelled nothing but sex juice. Netta pushed me off the couch and I landed on my feet on the hardwood floor. She scooted all the way down on the couch and put her legs all the way behind her head. She began to play with both her ass and pussy holes. I just stood there and enjoyed the show with my dick still coated with her mouth secretions. She fingered her pussy with two fingers and had a thumb up her butt. The double penetration was live and in fucking color. She was a real trooper to say the least.

"You like that baby? How that look to you?" She asked.

She worked both her holes while I sipped on my drink and enjoyed the live sex show. I even spit some liquor on her crotch to ensure wetness. The shit seeped from her pussy and rested on her asshole. She took her thumb and smeared the liquor infused saliva around both holes. That only made me spit more since she didn't protest in the first place. I kept sipping while she continued doing her thing.

"I do like this shit! You enjoying yourself ain't you?"

She was now jamming her thumb up her ass. This chick knew how to turn the party the fuck up! Seeing a woman violate herself can do a lot to you. It can turn your stomach if you not with the shit. Me, on the other hand, reacted in a totally different manner. My dick now was as hard as the stone pillars at the Roman Coliseum. The alcohol calmed me and kicked my freak notch up a bit. I looked down at my shit after taking another drink. I let some drink spill from my mouth onto my rod and the floor. I looked at her and she had her lips slightly parted. I took that as she needed more rod between her lips. I moved closer to her and squatted over her chest. While still holding my cup, I guided my dick into her mouth. I used no hands of course. I fucked her face with more aggression than earlier. Some of my monkey oil spilled on her flapping chest. I paid the mess no mind while my nut sack bounced to and fro off her slippery chin.

After several minutes of this, I pulled out and got up from the couch.

"You about to cum baby?" She asked opening her mouth wider.

"Nah. I'm nowhere near that point. I'm ready to move this show to another hole."

"Which one do you have in mind? You want my pussy or my ass?"

I had to take a long sip of my drink on that one. Never had I been offered my choice of entries into a woman's nether regions. Pussy and head were customary. Asshole was somewhat of an off the menu item. I done talked until I was blue in the face trying to get a chick to let me stick it where the sun never shines. Now I was faced with a game changing question. She was still playing with herself while waiting for my answer.

"I'll take door #2 please and thank you."

"Mmmm! Great choice! Now come on down and get your prize you sexy mufucka! Why was I waiting and hoping that your choice would be my ass! Come on over here and fuck my ass!"

A very cold chill washed over my entire body. I felt like I had the "Hi Pro Glow" or some shit. For some reason, the song by Dru Hill, "Sleeping In My Bed", was on repeat in my head. I took another sip and noticed that my cup was getting low. I refreshed my potion and moved closer to her. Netta pulled some lube from out of nowhere. She applied a healthy portion to her asshole. She stuck her thumb back in her ass to show me where I was to insert my dick. I grabbed a pillow from her bed and tossed it on the floor. I then knelt down on it and zeroed in on her anus. I took a condom and applied it to my member. She held both her ass cheeks open to clear the runway to her asshole. I inched closer to my target. I clicked the chain on the lamp next to the couch to shed light on the situation. Her asshole looked like a tiny mouth hanging open and begging for dick. I put the cup down to focus. I took hold of my cock and guided him into her puckered ass. The lube made the insertion go off without a hitch. I watched my beef disappear inch by inch into her brim. I didn't force it. I finessed it. I had to look into her face for reaction sakes. Her eyes were closed and her mouth was open. My dick was more than half way gone by now. The tightness that I felt was beyond words. She gripped the back of the couch as she shifted her body. I pressed her thighs into her chest. I stroked in and out for a few seconds. I positioned myself so my balance was secure. Now I was free to slowly poke and prod as I pleased.

"Ah! Ah! Your dick is stretching my ass! Fuck man! Damn! I like how you taking your time with it! You acting like you know what you doing! Ah!" Netta moaned.

I plunged in all the way to my balls. I could feel her asshole throbbing. I held her ankles back so far until that they resembled earrings. I pulled my cock damn near out of her before diving back in. I repeated this over and over as she made animalistic noises.

"Ugh! Ugh! Agh! Agh! Damn! This dick feels good Terry! You fucking me so good right now! You about to make my pussy cum with all that dick up my ass! Shit!"

She played with her pussy while I fucked her ass. She began to squirm as I intensified my strokes. I tried to hold her in place but she broke free. That left me holding one leg. She swung her free leg back and forth in the air. I put her leg on my shoulder and leaned forward. She was now on her side facing me. I took my hand and played with her lonely clit. I rubbed her meaty pussy lips and the wetness was very real. I pinned her securely against the back of the couch. Now I started to dig deep in her cunt.

"You like that? That ass is tight! Fuck! Shit feeling way too good! You just don't know how I'm feeling right now! Fuck! This shit is crazy!"

I drank from my cup and put it back down. Some of my alcohol spilled on her boobs. I felt as if I was having one of those experiences where you have stepped outside your body. I was on the bed watching myself with Netta. Her grunts turned me on every time I heard them. I held on to her leg for dear life eventually getting a hold to her loose leg. My grip tightened around her ankles as I pressed them against the couch. This ensured that I was now back in control of our little fuck fest.

"Holy fuck Terry! You so deep up my ass! That dick gone tear something up in me! Goddamn! I ain't have no dick in my ass for a minute! Your shit is brick too! That hard mufucka all the way in that ass! Let me hold my legs for you."

We traded possession of her ankles and I leaned back so I could watch the in and out movements between us. Her asshole turned inside out with every stoke. The cum from her pussy mixed perfectly with the lube. I stuck my finger back into her pussy hole. I could feel my dick inside her optional tunnel. Double penetration at its finest. I drank more liquor straight from the bottle. Again I spit all over her genital region.

"Shit! That shit burns! Fuck baby! You fucking the shit out of my tiny asshole! You trying to make me go crazy or some shit? I done came twice already! Damn! Spitting that drink on me is making me even hornier! How you liking this tight shit? Do you feel my body trembling? That's your dick doing all this to me! See what the fuck you doing to me? I didn't think you were gone fuck me like this!"

Her eyes rolled back as she bit her bottom lip. Her cheeks inflated and deflated with each breath. I was beginning to grow tired of our current position. I pulled out and stood up. I took another swig from the bottle as I gathered my thoughts. I decided to have her get on all fours on the floor in front of the couch. It was now time to get creative on her ass. I took her hands and put them on her ass. I then had her spread her ass cheeks as far as they could stretch. I let more cognac spill down her crack and onto the floor. Her body flinched as it crept down her anal crevice. I stood over her and took my position on the couch. I balanced myself on the bed as well. I had my hands on the bed and my feet on the couch. My dick was stiff enough to guide into her ass minus my hands. Her anus welcomed my pole once again. There was no holding back this time. Once my dickhead was immersed into her, I slammed the rest of me into her forcefully.

"Ah! What the fuck are you doing to me Terry? You all over this on your acrobat shit! Who you think you are fucking me like I belong to you? You trying to make me yours?"

She was talking really insane now. That shit was zooming by me. That shit wasn't even making it to my ears! I wasn't trying to hear none of that bullshit! She was not in her right state of mind. I guess she would say just about anything with a stiff one up her ass.

"Shut the fuck up! That ass gripping me so tight! Shit feeling real decent!"

"Decent? Nigga this ass A-1! I know my shit fire! Aw shit! You got me coming again! Damn baby! Your dick seems like it's only getting harder! Fuck me Terry! Your young ass got me going for real boy! I can get used to this here! Damn Terry! I like this dick! How you all up in the air over me fucking? Your back strong, huh?"

The drink had me feeling no pain. I clinched my butt cheeks and started pounding on her ass like a bongo.

"Damn! You trying to kill me or something? Goddamn! You fucking this ass ain't you? Why you keep making me cum so much?"

By now, the music in my head was on full blast. "Sleeping In My Bed" was still playing, but it was now the remix version. It was wrong for me to be fucking the next man's woman, but I'm sure that somebody was definitely somewhere returning the favor with my so called girlfriend. Karma works like that. I didn't have time to worry about the universe at the moment. This asshole thing was new to me. I had pussy before, but this was a whole new ballgame. The visual with her fingers in her pussy and my dick sliding in and out her bung hole was freaking me out in the best way. I could get used to that kind of action, but I damn sure was not about to utter a single word.

"My legs getting tired Terry. Lets switch this thing on up shall we? I know you would like to rest for a minute or two."

"What do you have in mind?" I asked still pumping away.

"I want to sit on your dick. I can face you or do the reverse cowgirl position. Either way, I want to ride it. You ain't got a problem with that do you?"

"Why would I? Let's keep this thing going!"

I pulled out her ass and waited for her to get up off the couch so I could sit. Her asshole was steady throbbing. That turned me on a tad bit more. I plopped down as soon as she got up. I did a quick rubber check to see if I was still covered. The check confirmed that I was indeed in good shape. She grabbed some lube and squirted some on her fingers. She ran her lubed digits up her ass for another round of action. I guess the appointed position was reverse cowgirl because she greased up her ass with her back to me. She put her feet up on the couch and squatted above my waiting rod. I was waiting on her to let me feel her vagina, but that wasn't about to happen. Back in her ass I went. She moved up and down with a slow motion grind. I just sat back while she did her thing. She rested her hands on the bed for more leverage. I watched closely as she fucked her own ass with the help of my cock. The sweat ran down her back and rested on her ass. I slapped her round backside as she rolled it on me. Her skin was smooth. She had some old school body art that really needed to be covered or erased completely. You know the kind that was created with a safety pin and a broken ink pen? Shit was so terrible that I could not even make it out for real. Her riding skills were more than decent. I love it when they raise damn near all the way off you then drop it all the way back down on you. That shit right there is the absolute truth! The grip that her ass had on me only intensified. Shit was so snug that if she would've got up she would've carried me on her back! Her soft ass cheeks slapped against my thighs. I gripped her shoulders to pull her into me with more force. I kept an eye on the rubber to make sure he was still in the game and he most definitely was. That mufucka was inching up my cock slightly though. I took a handful of her thick mane and that got her to bucking like a fool.

"Oh! Aw! Terry that's my shit! Pull my fucking hair! Shit! This dick ain't got soft yet!"

"Shut the fuck up and fuck me! It's your job to put this dick to bed! From the looks of it you slacking big time!"

"I see! The longer we fuck the stiffer it gets! Goddamn! You sure you ain't popped something in your drink or something when I wasn't looking? Niggas dicks don't get rock like this these days! How old you say you were? Boy, this dick taking me back to the 80's! Fuck my ass Terry! Fuck!"

Her accusation that I was on something struck a nerve deep within me. I don't take drugs to enhance my sexual prowess. How dare she! Before I knew it, I had poured my cup all over her head.

"Ah! Fuck Terry! That shit cold as fuck! You like to get messy huh? Shit!"

She was not outraged. She did not dismount from my lap either. Netta kept on humping despite having a back full of alcohol and wet hair. I had to smile at her savage ways. I took my hands off her ass and gave her double thumbs up salute behind her back.

"Keep doing your thing! Shit feeling way too good Netta!" I cheered her on.

"You like that Terry? You have no idea how you are making me feel right now! Let me readjust so you can hit another angle."

She turned sideways where we were almost facing each other. I was able to suck on her boob that tasted just like the alcohol I had just poured on her. She put her hand against my chest and rubbed my neck. I put my head back cause I'll be damned if she put her hand on my face after having them all up her coochie! I rubbed on her toned calves as her naked body gyrated. She dropped that ass and grinded deeply into my lap. The bird's eye view I had turned me on more. I smacked her ass as she continued to rock back and forth. She stared at me with her eyes all low and smoky looking. Nothing was said, just grunts and moans. I peered around the room that was littered with whatever you could name. Her closet door was securely shut and I really didn't think anything of it. Then it hit me. I had not fully inspected the killing floor before setting up shop. What the hell was I thinking? You should always look under beds and anywhere else where someone can be secretly hidden. I was no longer paying any attention to her ass riding my joint. My senses were now heightened. The door knob on that closet stood out to me. Maybe the drink was fucking with me. Netta was fake slick; but I wouldn't think she would toss me in a trick bag. Her daughter was in the next room or was she? I never saw her. I shook my head to get those thoughts out of my mental bank. I sat up a little and put my eyes back on her. She was back to juuging in her soggy twat. The room was dark and the moon was casting the perfect light. So perfect that the shadows outside were extremely animated. I could hear movement, but there was no reason for concern. My eyes and ears stayed peeled. I'm gazing at the closet door and meanwhile, something was walking up the back steps to the door that was in her room. The footsteps were loud and extremely clear.

"Hey! Somebody at the backdoor Netta!"

She was deep off in her zone. I had to pull her close so she could hear me.

"Huh? What you saying? Ain't nobody at my door!"

"I'm telling you that somebody outside!"

"Boy! Quit tripping! You acting paranoid like you off something!"

"Bang! Bang! Bang! Bang!" The imaginary being outside knocked at the door.

"Netta! Netta! Bitch! You see me calling your mufucking phone! I know your bitch ass up in there! What the fuck you in there doing that you can't answer me bitch? It bet not be no nigga in there either! Both of ya'll gone get fucked up! Bitch! Get your mufucking ass to this door bitch!"

"Oh shit! That's lil Joe! He crazy! I told him that I didn't want to fuck with him no more! Fuck!"

Netta jumped off my dick and started trying to find her clothes. I got my shit off the floor immediately. I didn't even have the words to express what I was feeling. I couldn't blame nobody but myself. This nigga was obviously sprung out over this fuck bucket ass freak! The fallen homies crossed my mind as the euphoric feeling escaped my body. She was moving around that room at the speed of light. My head swiveled back and forth between Netta in the room and lil Joe on the other side of the door. Anger entered my body as I got myself together. Something didn't smell right and it wasn't the sex in the air. I didn't know who was on what, so I pulled that iron from my waist. Netta came near me to do something and I couldn't help but to kick her in her lousy ass as hard as I could.

"What the fuck you doing Terry? Why you kick me up the ass for? Fuck! You know my shit still raw from fucking!"

I pointed my gun at her and then at the door. Then I directed it back towards her.

"Bitch! You on some snake shit! What the fuck!"

I hit her in her collar bone with the pistol to let her know shit was definitely real.

"Aaah! Shit! Man what are you doing? Don't kill me! Don't shoot me! Please Terry! I don't know why he out there! I didn't tell him to come!"

I hit her once again in a different part of her collar bone to even out her pain. I stuck the gun in her face as the tears flooded her eyes. I moved in closer and she cried louder. That angry dude was still out there bamming on the door. Now I could tell he was kicking at the door trying to break it down. Never would I let him force his way in on me. I cocked my shit and turned towards my enemy.

"Oh shit! What the fuck Terry! No!"

"Boom! Boom! Boom!" The .45 spoke up.

I had to let him know what was on the other side of that door. There were three nice holes in her shit. She was screaming like a fool as I made my way to her front door. I looked out the door on both sides of her crib.

"Boom! Boom!" It spoke up again.

I let off two more shots before I jetted to my ride. I preserved my ammo before I made it to the car just in case there happened to be some return fire. I jumped in my shit and started it up. I threw my gun on the seat and went into the console for my back up. I sat it on my lap as I scooted off down the one way street. I looked all around until I was back on Manchester. I ignored all the lights until I saw the highway. I was high speeding it back to the East Side. My phone rang and guess who it was?

"What up?"

"Yeah bitch ass nigga! This shit ain't over! Nigga you gone bust through the door at me? Cuzz you gone die for that one! You hear me cuzz?"

Was I hearing correctly? I know the nigga that I just shot at wasn't calling me from Netta's phone! What the fuck is that all about? I was not about to argue back and forth with a nigga who was lucky to even be alive. Hell! We both were cause that scene could have played out so much differently. I had to just shake my head and laugh it all off.

"Yo bro. It's all good. She's your bitch. She told me nothing about you dude. I would not have been there had I known about you. She's a cool chick. She's a little sneaky though. You might want to keep a better eye on her. Be cool bro," I said ending the call.

He hit my line as soon as I hung up. Guess he wanted to get the last word. I kept ignoring him until I couldn't take it no more. I decided to answer one last time.

"Sup!"

"Yeah this that nigga lil Joe! Aye bruh. I want to ask you a question."

"Aite. I'm listening."

"Oh? You mean to tell me that this bitch didn't tell you that I was her nigga? Is that what you telling me?"

"That's what I'm telling you. She said that her man was overseas. I had no idea that she was dealing with anyone besides him. I just met her today. Look, I'm finna get off of here and leave you two to have a blessed night."

"Aye bruh. Can you answer just one more question?"

"What is it man?"

Now he was softening his tone and speaking as if he had some sense. That still didn't negate the fact that he did indeed just threaten to take my life.

"I know we grown and all, but I have to ask. What was ya'll in here doing? She said that ya'll was just in here chilling and drinking. Bitch said nothing was going on. She said you some lame she felt sorry for. What's up man? Give it to me raw. What the fuck was ya'll doing?"

That shit he was saying forced me to laugh. The little credit I gave her was now all used up. Netta was a trip and a half.

"Well bruh. I don't kiss and tell, but since I didn't kiss her here it goes. I was drinking while she was attempting to eat me alive. Her head was noteworthy. That's probably why you on my line. Couldn't tell you what that pussy hitting on cause I was too busy up the bitch asshole!"

"What! Da fuck!"

All I heard was the phone drop to the floor followed by loud screams and what I could've sworn were blows to Netta's face and body.

"Smack!"

"Bitch! You letting this goofy ass nigga fuck you all in your funky ass huh?"

"No Joe! He lying! I didn't do shit! Fuck what he talking about! You know how I feel about you baby!"

"Pop! Slap!"

"Bitch! That nigga just fired on me over your stupid ass! I'm gone fuck you up in this bitch!"

"Joe! Please! You said you wasn't gone hit me no more! Please Joe!"

I listened until I had heard enough. Her lying had caught up with her in the worst way. Dude was regulating her but that had nothing to do with me. I was thankful to be in one piece. As far as I was concerned, the night was a success. I got my first shot of asshole and was thirsty for more. I crossed the MLK bridge with the rubber still on my dick in search of more action for the night that had just begun.

Chapter 4
Tough Ass

"Girl stop at the Arab spot so we can get a cigarillo. I'm ready to get high cause ain't nothing shaking tonight," said Cake.

"Alright bitch. It is dead for real. These niggas ain't on shit," said Racquel.

"My phone dry as old lady pussy. We need to hit the road if we want to get into some real shit."

Racquel pulled into the parking lot of the gas station in Washington Park on Kingshighway. As she got out the car, she noticed two guys arguing. She couldn't hear them at first, so she walked closer cause she was nosey as fuck.

"Nigga! Didn't I tell you about trying to play games with me? You must think I'm a bitch or something?" The larger cat barked.

"Nah Mark man! I was gone call you but I lost my phone! You know I wouldn't do you like that!"

The big dude stole him clean in his face. He kept on beating him until he was on the ground. Big dude picked him up by the neck and carried him to the car. He held him with one hand and popped the trunk with the other one.

"What you doing man? Nah man! Please!" The guy begged.

The big dude said no more as he lifted him into the trunk and shut the lid. He looked over at Cake who was all up in his business. She couldn't help but to stare back at him.

"What you looking at? You know me?" He asked.

"Should I know you? Shit! You looking all crazy at me!"

He moved closer to this interesting young lady who definitely wasn't intimidated by his menacing demeanor. He sized up her 5'5" 160lb frame that was packed into skin tight True Religion jeans and a t-shirt to match. She was high yellow and sassy/jazzy as fuck. Her micro braids looked as if she had just got out of the African's chair on 22nd and State St. He could damn near see his reflection in her teeth when she smiled.

"I'm looking at you cause you all up in my shit! I'm Mark. What do you go by sexy lady?"

"My name is not sexy lady!" Cake snapped.

"Oh my bad! Sorry about that! I just call 'em like I see 'em! What's your name? If you don't mind me asking."

"Now that's better. My name is Cake. Nice to meet you Mark. I just love me a man who works for a living. You do have a job don't you Mark? I mean, you are dressing the part."

She was referring to the khaki Dickie outfit he sported.

"I work at the shoe factory up the way. So since I do have a job, can I ask for your number so I can take you out sometimes?"

"Nah, you can't have my number. You can give me yours though. I'll call you if I feel like being bothered."

Mark laughed at her remarks. He couldn't believe how cocky she was after seeing what she just saw. Cake already had her phone in her hand waiting on him.

"You ready? It's (618) 972 – 03," he told her.

"Alright I got you locked in. We about to get in the wind."

"What ya'll about to get into?"

"Damn you kind of nosy ain't you?"

Mark laughed, "Nah, it's nothing like that at all. I was just asking for real. I see ya'll got cigarillos. That means somebody is a smoker. Wait right here."

The girls looked at each other while Mark fumbled around in his car. After a few seconds, he came out with a plastic sandwich bag full of exotic herb.

"Here you go. Ya'll can smoke on that," he said.

He handed her the baggie. Cake just looked at Mark who was now smiling.

"So you just gone let me get this? What is this going to cost me? I'm not about to accept something without knowing the terms."

"Why you can't just take the blessing and gone on? Every nigga ain't out to get you. You bad and all, but I was just trying to help you blow a little better. I just took it as a blessing and I'm passing it on. Now you tell me what's up?"

"What you want for it? I can't just take shit out here for free. Put a tag on it and I got you."

"Oh! You moving like that? I see what's up! Well give me $100 for it and it's yours. Does that work for you?"

"You want $100 for all this? It's well over an ounce in here! You doing it like that? Oh shit! I'm scared of you boy! You know you doing the most right now! You mean to tell me that you gone give me $400 worth of tree for $100? What is the catch?"

"You tripping girl! I was just giving it to you. You the one making it out to be more than what it is. You need to gone break me off that change before you miss out on this once in a lifetime deal!"

Cake laughed while unzipping her Gucci fanny pack. She pulled out a decent knot and peeled off a big faced hundred dollar bill.

"I like that pouch on your waist lil mama. Where you get that from? Don't tell me you fucking with Hood's lot mall like the rest of these broke ass shit talking hoes!"

Mark's statement pissed Cake off to the highest degree. Hood's lot was a flea market area on Kingshighway in East St. Louis. That's where all the knockoff/bootleg shit comes from.

"Nigga! You got me fucked up! This pouch comes straight out the Gucci store in Frontenac, Mo. If it ain't official, it ain't me! I don't fuck with nothing fugazi! As a matter of fact, you want a bill right? Well fuck it! Here go $200! Just so you know what it is over here!"

Cake shoved two big face hundreds in Mark's hand. She smirked at him for coming at her sideways in the first place. His insult netted him another hundred.

"You a lil stunter huh? I see money ain't a problem on your end. I'll go buy me something nice with it. Thanks!"

"Yeah whatever! We about to leave from here. I don't want to keep you from doing whatever it is you about to do," Cake said.

She winked and nodded towards the trunk. Mark did not catch on at first, but when he did, all he could do was giggle.

"I see you have a sense of humor. I'll hopefully hear from you later. Be safe and stay sexy."

"You too bae."

They split and went to their cars. There was so much noise on the busy lot that no one could hear dude in the trunk crying out for help. To make it more real, there was a Washington Park squad car sitting on the lot the entire time! Mark pulled off slow and turned his sounds all the way up to drown the screams from his cargo. Cake got back in the car and placed the weed in her lap.

"Bitch! Where that come from? You didn't have that before you got your ass out this car! What did I miss?" Racquel quizzed.

Cake broke down the cigar and began to fill it with potent reefer. She didn't even bother to break it down. She rolled it and dried it with the lighter. She lit it and passed it to Racquel without even hitting it first.

"Here bitch! You need to smoke and calm the fuck down!"

Racquel took the blunt and pulled on it. The sweet smoke entered her lungs and caused her to cough uncontrollably as she exhaled.

"Shit! That shit right here is nothing to fuck with! This way better than that weed floating around the city. How you come up on this sack girl?"

"Your ass stay in somebody business. You need to cut that bullshit out girl. If you have to know, I got it from old boy on the lot I was talking to."

"You mean the big dude who put the other dude in the trunk? What the fuck are you doing? He just gone give you all this weed for nothing?"

"No bitch! I didn't get it for nothing! I paid him for it! Don't worry, we good girl. I made sure that we were covered."

"I'm just saying girl. He look like he don't play. I ain't trying to be next to old boy he put in the trunk!" Racquel said.

"Girl quit tripping! You making too much out of nothing! I told you we good. We about to blow lovely while we ride through this raggedy mufucka! Good I bought more than one 'rillo cause we smoking personals. I don't want you worrying. I want to see you high as the sky. Matter of fact, let's hit the Lou and gas up. We chilling today."

Cake proceeded to roll another blunt as Racquel sped towards the Eads Bridge by way of downtown. They ended up at the gas station off highway 70 and Grand Ave. Cake went in to pay for the gas. She ended up with cups of ice, more cigarillos, and a fifth of Bombay Sapphire Gin. She got in the car and began pouring up immediately before lighting her blunt.

Racquel got in and said, "Damn! You trying to get all the way in the clouds huh? Pour some more of that Mr. Pure in my shit too! Shit looking clear as fuck! You know how I feel about that damn gin! Where are we headed to?"

"Girl we just floating and trying to see what's what. It's a nice day so we need to enjoy it."

With that said, they were off. Cats were blowing at them at every light trying to get their attention. They were two sexy young ladies riding in a new Mercedes CLS 550 thang. They hit the dope and laughed while listening to old school tunes on the satellite radio. Both of their phones rang off the hook the whole time. They decided to stop at the Best Steak House for a quick bite to eat. Cake ordered the gyro plate while Racquel settled on the chicken. As they got their drinks, they both looked and noticed a familiar face in the place. It was Mark. He was in there pigging out on a t-bone steak.

"You see that nigga? Let's go fuck with him," Cake said as they made their way to his table.

"What's up ladies? How ya'll doing? I see ya'll on what I'm on. Great minds think alike huh? Have a seat."

"We just seen you. You move mad fast huh? You here by yourself?"

"Why wouldn't I be by myself? I don't fuck with these fuck niggas! I move by my lonesome, but I'm not lonely. Feel me?" Mark said with a flirty wink.

He was such a gentleman. That made it next to impossible to resist his charm. They just witnessed him trunking someone. Now they were sitting at the table together breaking bread.

"Ya'll come here often? They food pretty decent," Mark stated.

"We mostly come after catching a show at the Fox Theater across the street. We were in the area so we stopped in. They never let you down in this spot!"

"Where are my manners? I'm Mark and you are?"

He spoke in reference to never making Racquel's acquaintance. He wiped his hands on his napkin before extending his hand to her.

"I'm Racquel. Nice to meet you Mark," she said shaking his hand.

Mark eyed her beauty. Racquel had shoulder length hair that was cut to a tee. Her face was topped to perfection by it. Her coffee colored skin shined with no makeup. The lip gloss she wore drew attention to not only her lips, but her straight white teeth. She was built like the ex athlete that she happened to be. Her body was designed specifically to make men salivate in her presence. Mark had to catch his self cause that's exactly what he was doing. The two young ladies looked tastier than the steak on his plate.

"Nice to meet you Racquel. Two beautiful women sitting with me. Ya'll making me feel important. Where ya'll men at before I get too comfortable? I know ya'll got some fleas on your asses that refuse to let go!" He laughed.

"Don't get us started on these so called men these days!" Cake responded.

Racquel nodded in approval.

"Yeah, it's something terrible out here! You just don't know the half!" Racquel tossed her two cents into the discussion.

"Huh? What ya'll getting at? Let a slow brother catch up!"

"Well, let's just say that men expect way too much but give way too little," Cake said.

Her statement caused Mark's entire face to ball up as he carefully cut his steak.

"I'm listening," he said as he chewed his medium rare piece of meat.

"Like, I don't ask nobody for nothing. I was taught how to get money by the best of them. I don't need a nigga for shit! I know how to take care of me. I do get lonely though. I like to go on dates and outings just like the next chick. Feel what I'm saying? However, all I ask is for you to let me know what it is before our feelings get involved. I'm a woman before I'm anything. Just tell me your situation and let me decide if I want to deal with you or not," Cake said.

Mark sipped his water before asking, "So what do you mean by all that?"

"What she means is we don't do drama of any kind Mark! We need to know about your wife, baby mama, girlfriend, boo, or whatever you have going on upfront. It's always better to let somebody know your situation first off. Ain't nobody got time to be playing with grown people. Just say what you mean and mean what the fuck you say!"

Mark paid attention to the way the young women spoke for one another. That small fact intrigued the hell out of him.

"So do ya'll always move together like this? I mean, ya'll speaking like a unit or something. Ya'll twins? I applaud your unity. You know teamwork makes the dream work!" Mark laughed with his mouth full of steak of potatoes.

The ladies cringed at the gross sight. It was rude as hell to have your mouth full and to also have it hanging wide open.

"Yes, we move together as a team. We have learned over the years that we are all we got," Racquel explained.

"Uh man! Don't start with that dumb ass bullshit! Don't get me started with that wore out ass line!" Mark said with a straight face.

They both gave him a look. Mark saw their faces and was not moved at all. They went silent, so something needed to be said to calm the uneasiness at their table.

"What? Did I say something ya'll don't like? If you got something to say, get it off your chest! What's up?"

Mark leaned back in his seat and threw his hands up.

"Nah. You saying all the right shit if you trying to get your ass fucked up in this bitch! Is that the outcome you looking for Mark? I have no problem coming across this table! Now what's up?" Cake said as she threw her napkin down.

"Hmmm! I like that kind of shit! I meant no disrespect. I just get tired of that we all we got bullshit. That shit dead for real. I like the way you are standing up. Shit is kind of sexy if you ask me."

Instead of striking fear into Mark, her words did just the opposite. He was actually getting turned on by their exchange. He was sadistic in that way.

"Sexy? What you mean?" They both said confused.

"Let me explain without someone coming across the table on me please. It's sexy how you speak the truth. I say the same thing. I love to put shit on the table so to speak. You will never have to guess what I'm thinking. I don't have time to be bullshitting with people. We all grown at the end of the day; so let it be what it's gone be. Is that better ladies?" Mark said with a smile.

"Yeah whatever nigga. Sounds like somebody scared. You hear this nigga copping pleas Racquel? We got him shook in the worst way! Look at him girl!"

They all laughed while the ice was broken and melting away. They were giving Mark all the right signals. He had to pay attention to his hand and play the right card at the right time. He held no cut cards, so he was bound to say whatever whenever.

"Who scared?" Mark asked looking behind him.

They pointed at him while flashing goofy grins. The alerts on their phones caused their attention to be diverted to their screens. Text messages were sent and phones went back on the table. They laughed at the flip phone that Mark sported proudly.

"What the fuck is that? That bitch is a dinosaur! Where you did that up from?" Racquel laughed as she texted on her I-Phone.

"Oh? You tripping off my lil hitter huh? I happen to fuck with this heavy! I'm old school. I don't need them fancy phones. All I need to do is get my calls. Now ain't that what they for? Who I got to impress? Nobody! Half the people I see with them can't afford them no way! Texting over the wifi and talking with them free apps! Nah I'm cool. I keep it simple. Ya'll some fancy people if you ask me. I don't even know why ya'll sat with my basic ass. See I'm uncomfortable now! Ya'll happy?"

The girls busted out laughing again. That was a sure sign that the comfort level was achieved. Mark smiled on the inside because they had no idea that they were being sized up for an impromptu visit to the killing floor. The hunt was definitely underway whether the ladies were aware or not.

"You don't look uncomfortable to me Mark. You sitting over there like you used to being in the company of more than one bad bitch at a time. That's how you rolling dude? You think you can handle us? Hmmm?"

Cake tossed out the challenge. The door was now cracked and Mark was getting ready to kick that mufucka off the damn hinges! A big dumb ass grin covered his face as he wiped his mouth.

"Excuse me ladies. I was just wondering if I heard you correctly. Can I handle you both? I was thinking more like could you two handle me? I ain't no baby sitter!"

"So what you getting at boy? Don't be writing checks that you can't cover! You hear this dude? He trying to flex on us! He better check our resumes if he wants some trouble! You think he ready Cake?"

"I don't know, but he sure is talking like he wants war!" Cake chimed in.

"Writing checks? Where they do that at? I don't know about other people, but I only deal with cash!" Mark said slamming down a few racks on the table.

Now shit was getting serious. Mark glared at the ladies waiting on their comeback. He wasn't waiting for long cause they went in their pockets too.

"Nigga we ain't writing any checks over here either!" Cake said.

She slammed her bankroll on the table. Racquel followed suit as well. They had to laugh at the sight of over ten thousand between them. Mark was now in heaven. Don't nothing get a nigga dick harder than a bad ass; get money, never petty ass bitch!

"Oh! So you holding like that huh? Ya'll got me feeling a certain type of way right now! My dick hard enough to lift this table off the floor!"

"You just say whatever huh? This paper got you turned on like that? Damn! Most niggas will say it's the two bad bitches sitting here, but you a different breed. Money makes his dick hard! Imagine that shit! Nigga ain't after no pussy! He wants the money! Now that makes my cat get wetter than a river duck trapped in the rain!"

"Damn! I like the sound of that! My dick just got a little harder on that note! Some fine ass bitches who about that paper! Whoo! You talking about some wet pussy! What about you? What's the current situation of your crotch? Hmmm?"

Mark turned his attention to Racquel.

She smiled, "Well, if you really need to know. My pussy stays soggy as a sponge in a bucket full of water. Is that fine with you?"

That was music to his ears. Now the game was underway. The sexual tension was as thick as a bitch dancing at the Queen of Diamonds in Washington Park.

"So we got a hard dick and two wet pussies between us. What do ya'll propose we do about this? I'm ready to shake something. I've had dinner. Now I'm ready for some dessert. Would you like to help me out with something sweet?"

"A sweet tooth huh? Mmm! Maybe, just maybe we can make something crack. I don't know. What you think Racquel?"

"Hmmm. It's with me. I'm not trying to be on no disappointed shit either. This pussy too good to waste on some bullshit! Niggas be tripping on some other shit!"

"What you mean?" Mark asked immediately.

Racquel looked at Cake and then back to Mark.

"Niggas dick game don't be hitting on jack shit these days! Half of them can't get hard, can't stay hard, or just can't fuck period!"

"I know that's right!" Cake added slapping high five with her partner in crime.

"I don't fall into none of them slots. I'm thinking about both of you for my dessert," Mark announced.

"Oh? You ready for all of this?" Racquel smiled.

She stood up to let Mark survey the merchandise. She spun around so he could get a full view. He checked her out with a crazy look on his face. She was well put together, but he knew she was more than outstanding outside of her clothes. That caused him to giggle on top of his smirk.

"What's so damn funny? You see all this in front of you? Boy don't play! Girl he ain't ready!"

"It's only one way to find out. I don't think ya'll ready for real cause ya'll doing a lot of talking. I don't see no action though! "

Mark tossed the hot potato back into their lap with that one.

"Believe me! It's plenty action behind every word we speak dude! Ain't nobody got time to be going back and forth with you!"

Mark began gathering his paper and preparing to leave the packed eatery.

"Well, you are aware of what state we happen to be in right? I am all about expensive actions. I avoid cheap words. I want both ya'll tonight if you not scared. Ya'll talking about how wet your pussies are. I'm talking about how hard my dick is. To me that sounds like a nice mix. Now if you want to try me, you can call me later and see what's up. All I have to do is wrap up some business from earlier then I'll be free. If you want to test the water, holla at me. If not, shut the fuck up and stop wasting my time. Hear me? Now if you ladies would excuse me. I need to raise on up out of here," Mark said getting up from the table.

Sensing the challenge, Cake jumped out the window. Never would she allow anyone, especially a man, to get the last word over her.

"What? Nigga who bluff you trying to call? Ain't no weak bitches around here! What the fuck wrong with you? You acting like someone scared of your ass! Psst!"

Cake sounded salty/insulted. Reverse psychology is a mufucka ain't it? Mark had her ass exactly where he wanted her. Too bad her cocky ass was too consumed with her bullshit ego to see she was headed full speed into the trap Mark set since they sat down!

"Well ain't nothing to do but the damn thang! If that pussy good as the shit you talk, we might be able to twerk something! Hear me?" Mark said.

"Boy you must not know me! Ain't nobody talking shit but you! I just hope that dick as hard as you trying to act! Now hear that!"

The ladies rose up from the table and stood with their hands in the air. Now they were engaged in a full on standoff. There wasn't anything left to do but what they were talking about in the first place.

"I got a spot on the south side of the city. Let me give you the directions so you can bring your big mouth asses over!"

He gave them the info and all was set in motion.

"I know where this shit at. I know my way around this bitch. You gone be there at what time with that weak ass dick? What you need for us to bring?"

Cake's straightforward attitude kept Mark's attention. He liked a bad bitch with a slick mouth. At this particular time, he was in the company of two. No one was intimidated or backing down. It could be nothing short of an epic night.

"You don't let up do you? You just go hard at all times huh? I love that shit by the way. Ya'll some real bitches and I definitely respect that. I have a good feeling in my gut about you two. I don't invite bitches over every day. Real people are hard to come by. I appreciate that you offered to bring something over. I have everything you may need at the crib. Whatever you need, I got! All you need to bring is them soggy ass pussies! Hear me? I'll see ya'll in about an hour or so. Does that work for ya'll? Now gone tell your boyfriends that you will see them tomorrow. I'm on some kidnap shit tonight!"

"I ain't telling nobody shit! What the fuck I look like checking in with a lame ass nigga? Fuck outta here! You just have your funny looking ass there!"

Mark shook his head at her sassy attitude.

"I feel you man. I'll be there shortly. Make sure you nice and clean too! I like my pussy smelling like Fiji water. Hear me?"

Racquel reached in her pants and grabbed a handful of her own pussy. She took her hand out of her crotch and ran her fingers across his nose. Mark inhaled her sweetness and closed his eyes.

"You like that? That's what you over here wolfing about? My shit stays fresh! You smell me?"

Cake nodded her head as Mark's face told the story without his lips ever moving.

"Well you gone and handle your business. We will be ready whenever you are," Cake said.

"Shit! I'm on my way right now!" Mark said in a hurry.

"We'll call you shortly. Make sure them balls ain't got no salt on them! Alright?"

Mark laughed as he stuck his hand down his boxers. He put his hand to his nose as the girl's looked on.

"Eww! You so nasty!"

"You could say that. I'm just me though. Hit me in about 45 minutes. I'm outta here!" Mark said.

He jumped into a different whip than the one he was in earlier. The girl's got into their car and smoked some more. They decided to take it easy on the drink since they were set to meet Mark within the next hour. They were feeling good with their stomachs on decent.

"Girl I'm high as gas prices! I'm feeling kind of freaky right now. We gone see what he talking about real soon," Cake said texting on her phone.

"I know what you mean bitch. He's an old funny looking ass nigga too! Swear he that deal too! You know what though?"

"What girl?"

"It be them niggas you ain't really attracted to that surprise the hell out of you!"

"I know right! His chubby ass acting like he gone kill something! He keeps you laughing though. That's what makes you want to see what's up with him. Talking about his dick and shit! He throwed the fuck off if you ask me! Them type of niggas go hard for real. He doesn't look like much but his confidence has me curious. I sound real stupid right now; but you know what I'm talking about."

"Yeah whatever bitch. What time is it? How much time done passed since we been sitting here talking shit?" Racquel inquired.

Neither one of them had been paying the time much attention. Smoking high powered reefer while discussing sex can consume a person. Cake squinted at her phone while trying to figure out how long they had been there. After she couldn't get a grip on the situation, she decided to scroll through her previous texts.

"Damn!"

"What girl? What time is it?"

"Bitch it's been over an hour!"

"You lying! How long has it been?"

"We been sitting for damn near two hours!"

They both sat quietly in the smoggy car for a few moments. Smoking high powered reefer, texting, and shooting the shit can be very time consuming if you are not careful.

"Let me text him to see if it's still on and popping. He probably in the wind right now," Cake said texting Mark.

Racquel puffed on her blunt in the meantime. Cake sent the text and her phone rang soon after.

"Hello and how may I help you Mr. Mark?"

"I should be asking you that! Don't tell me ya'll got a better offer and calling to break the news to me!" He laughed.

"Nah nigga. It ain't even like that. We lost track of time. I really blame your ass!"

"How do you blame you, I mean me?"

He responded so fast that he jumbled his words.

"Shit! If you had never gave us that damn weed we would've been there already!"

"Oh ok! I see how you are! You wild style for that one. Never heard that one before. I guess I am if you say I am."

"Whatever Eminem. What's your location? We about to fall on through if it's still a go."

Mark gave them directions and they listened closely.

"We need to freshen up once we get there. You got some clean towels and shit over there? You know how niggas get down," Racquel shouted in the background.

"I thought ya'll stay fresh? I got some shit for ya'll to clean your funky asses on up! I got you covered! Just bring your sexy selves over here!"

"We on our way! We'll be there in a flash," Cake confirmed before hanging up.

Racquel started the car and they pulled off slowly. They had to let the moonroof back so the car could air out. Mark didn't stay too far away; so they arrived at his place in a matter of minutes. They pulled up to the two family flat tucked away off Sidney Ave. It was a neat, brick situation that was freshly renovated. The lawn was cut to perfection which added to the curb appeal. The girls got out and walked up the steps to ring the bell. After several rings, Mark shuffled to the door.

"Who goes there? I say who goes there?"

"If you don't open this mufucking door! You know who the fuck it is!" Racquel blurted out.

Mark looked out the window located on the side of the over sized French door. He smiled when he saw what was staring back at him on his door step. He shook his head as he opened the door.

"How may I help you ladies? Ya'll must be lost or something?"

Mark stood in the door with a Calvin Klein robe and some Clark slippers on.

"Boy if you don't get your wide ass out the doorway!" Cake said pushing past him.

"Damn you just gone move me out the way huh? That's black folks for you!"

The girls walked in and immediately kicked off their shoes. They were amazed at how the outside of the house gave you no indication of what was inside. The hardwood floors shined as if there was a light underneath them. There was a spiral stair case in the center of the living area. The kitchen had stainless steel appliances and granite countertops. The wrap around cabinets were just as shiny as the floors. There was a large flat screen mounted over the fireplace. The furniture was suede, large, and extremely pristine. There was a portable bar with every genre of alcohol being represented in its top shelf form. There were a few jars full of reefer also. There was some Gap Band playing on the surround sound system. Mark walked to the makeshift bar and poured up three shots of Boca Patron. He handed the ladies a glass before picking up his own.

"Let's toast to a night that we won't soon forget," he said.

They all held their shot glasses in the air before clanging them together. Everybody took their shot down in one gulp. That prompted Mark to pour them all another. They then repeated the routine once again. The warm alcohol calmed their nerves completely.

"Damn nigga! You trying to get us twisted before the night even kicks off!" Cake said with a balled up face.

"I make it customary for my guests to take a shot as soon as they enter my home. Don't even trip ladies. It's all good!"

"Hey! Where can we wash up?" Cake asked looking around.

"Ya'll can use the restroom down here or you can go to the one upstairs. It's got a tub, shower, two sinks, and what not," he told them in a nonchalant way.

Racquel caught his stunting off rip, "You hear this nigga? If I didn't know no mufucking better! Let me shut up!"

They shared a laugh once again. It's always a pleasure to be around people who can joke with one another without any offense being taken. Mark got more shots prepared while the ladies made their decision.

"I guess we can go upstairs and do what we need to do. Come on girl."

"I'll get ya'll some fresh towels and face rags. Don't want you washing your ass and face with the same rag so I'll put out two. Hear me?"

"Yeah we hear you. Make sure one of them rags white too!" Cake said smirking.

"The one for your face right? We don't want any stains on them Calvin Klein towels."

Mark began to walk up the spiral steps as the ladies fell in behind him. He walked to the master bedroom where the bathroom was located. He hit the light so they could see better.

There were his and hers sinks and a large Jacuzzi tub that could seat at least eight adults. There was also a glass shower with an overhead spout, a spout out the wall, a bench for sitting, and more room than your average shower.

The ladies took all this in and tried their best not to appear too impressed. They undressed as Mark got their towels and wash cloths out the closet.

"You sure you single? This here sure looks like you sharing space with somebody. I mean, you got all those feminine hygiene products on that side of the sink. Tell us something before we get all comfortable. I don't want to be caught off guard by one of your loose ass hoes!"

"Now why my hoes got to be loose? I can't deal with no one with sense huh? If all my hoes loose, what does that make ya'll? Answer me that one right quick since you seem to know all about my personal life!"

He successfully flipped their accusations right back on them. Their faces let him know that they were not ready for that at all.

"Boy bring our stuff so we can get ourselves together! Please and thank you kind sir!" Racquel said playfully, but serious at the same time.

She was standing there in her bra with her pants unzipped. Her undid Chanel belt was just dangling. That lil line of thin hair which led to the pussy was visible. The saliva was steady accumulating in Mark's mouth. His eyes diverted over to

Cake's unbuckled Gucci belt. Her La Perla underwear let you know that she was far from a basic bitch.

"Here you go. Clean them cats ladies! I'll be downstairs if you need me," Mark said.

He laid their towels down and walked towards the door.

"Come here Mark. Let me holla at you for a quick lil minute," Racquel beckoned.

Mark was jumping for joy on the inside, but keeping his cool demeanor on the outside.

"What's up? What you need?"

He stood before them in only his robe and slippers. Racquel undid his robe and it fell open. She smirked at his striped Calvin Klein boxers and solid black wife beater of the same name. The stiff cock print was right there for all to see. Mark had that closed mouth grin. Racquel went in his drawers and retrieved his hard wood. She smiled before looking down at it. Her and Cake unleashed globs of spit onto his dick before attacking it. Cake took the head and left the shaft to Racquel. Mark's eyes went to the ceiling as his head tilted backwards. The girls were extremely careful with his stiff member. They didn't treat it like bubble gum. They didn't suck too hard. They used the right amount of tongue.

"You feeling that? You like that? Mmmm!" Cake said looking at him in between slurps on his veiny meat.

"Fuck yeah I'm feeling that shit! How can I not? I'm digging the chewing! I love it! Ya'll be careful down there!" Mark warned.

"Why should we be careful? Hmmm?" Racquel asked swallowing his manhood to the balls.

"Shit! The reason I say that is because my shit hard as cement right now!"

"Exactly! What we need to be careful for? It should be full speed ahead!" Cake asked.

"I'm not paying no dental bill for no cosmetic surgery that you may need!"

"What the fuck I'm gone need that shit for?" Racquel asked while tickling his balls with her tongue.

"Shit! Hard as my dick is you fuck around and chip a tooth or something! I'm just letting you know what it is way in advance!"

The girls laughed at his crazy ass. Here he was with two bitches on his cock and balls and still finding time to crack jokes.

"Nigga you got problems for real! Anybody told you that before? Fucking crazy ass boy! Get on up out of here! We'll be down shortly," Cake said pushing him out the door.

"I can tell when I'm not needed! Ya'll need something just holla. I may holla back. Who knows?"

"Whatever nigga! Bye!" Cake said still laughing.

Mark left as the ladies washed their "hot spots." They made sure not to use soap in their special places. Niggas like you to be fresh, but not that soap taste on the vagina. That is not the best mixture if you want your pussy eaten. If you got a taste for soap; you might as well eat a bar of soap and say, "Fuck that pussy!"

They finished in the bathroom and walked out. They noticed Mark sitting on the plush couch as they descended the winding stairs. He was jacking his dick and drinking liquor. He was definitely on some animal shit. The girls couldn't believe that he had no shame.

"Damn nigga! You couldn't wait for us to get the party started?" Racquel asked walking towards him.

Mark stared at them with his poker face on stuck. He had more shots poured for them. There was powder and various pills present also.

"What the fuck you on dude? You on some getting your nose dirty type shit? We don't fuck around with no damn cocaine or heroin or none of that shit!" Cake affirmed quickly.

"My my my! So damn defensive! Chillax girl! You getting all crazy for nothing! First off, that ain't nothing but some Molly. I have it on display for a reason. Any other nigga would've put that shit in your drink and not said a word. I don't play games with people."

The girls' eyebrows went up as they looked at the ready made drinks. Mark saw this and grabbed them and threw them both back. They all smiled as their apprehensions were put to rest. Mark poured two more plus another one for himself. He raised his glass and the girls did also.

"To a good night with good people. Cheers!" Mark toasted.

They clanked their glasses and took their shots.

"That's right," Racquel added.

"Here here," Cake said.

They sat on the couch and vibed to old school tunes. The girls danced in the seated position.

"If ya'll want to dance for me, I don't mind. I'll just sit here and mind my business," Mark said half grinning.

The drinks were doing their job on the women's inhibitions. The table they sat their glasses on had dildos and lube on display. The girls knew they had stepped off into a real vagarious situation. Mark got up from the couch and walked to get to the bottle from the counter. He was now sipping minus the shot glass. His eyes were getting lower by the minute. His vision was blurred, but the clear target was the two half naked ladies in his living room.

"Ya'll want some more drink?"

"Yeah that's cool," they answered simultaneously.

More drinks were poured as the girls eyed the freak kit on the table. They then looked at one another. Mark quickly caught on to what they were doing.

"What ya'll looking at?"

"This table full of fake dicks and ass grease! Shit! What you think we looking at?" Cake spit.

"You got something against these toys? They ain't done nothing to you. At least not yet anyway!" Mark chuckled.

"Shit nigga! I don't have anything against no toys! I just prefer the real thing if you want the truth! You got a real dick on you don't you? That mufucka was hard upstairs! Don't tell me you one of these niggas that can't stay hard! Don't tell me that bullshit! That shit will blow all highs for real!" Racquel ranted.

"Super Freak" by Rick James played as the temperature rose between the occupants of the room.

"Yeah don't tell me you ain't built for this here. We on some real grown folks shit. All the babies been put to bed already you know. I see you still up, so I guess you not no baby, huh?" Cake joked.

Mark just sat there smiling. The girls had no idea what they were in for. They had stepped off in the gladiator arena with a real lion. He took a swig straight from the bottle.

"Aww! This that shit right here! Just how freaky are you two? Hmmm? How loose ya'll trying to get? Hmmm? I don't think ya'll with shit for real. Scary ass hoes just blowing hot air!"

Mark mean mugged the girls so they could see how serious he was.

"Well, we can get down with you, but not each other if that's what you are wanting. I'm not into girls, but other than that, its whatever," Cake said.

"I like bitches, but not this one. We like family for real. I'm not against too much else though. What you have in mind for us?" Racquel asked smiling.

Mark passed the bottle to the girls and they each took a sip then back to Mark it went. Everybody had their eyes stuck on low.

"What's the freakiest shit ya'll done did? Don't say ass fucking either cause that be normal shit!"

They had to think for a minute.

"Hmmm. Well, I done had three ways before," Cake said.

"Basic. What about you?" He said cutting her off.

"Probably a three way with two dudes," Racquel said.

"Bitch! That's a lightweight train right there!" Mark laughed.

"Nigga! What's up? What are we on tonight? I guess you got something up your sleeve. Well? You gone let us know or what? We waiting nigga!" They both challenged.

"Drum roll please. You see them dildos right there? Well, I prefer that strap on joint right here. This bitch serious you hear me? Mufucka gone get the job all the way done!"

"Oh! So you would rather use the strap on than your real dick nigga? Your shit was pretty hard before. What you need the phony meat for?"

Mark got a bottle of Avion tequila and drank more from the bottle. The night was cranking to the point where the glasses were no longer necessary. The girls had the Silver Patron.

"What's the dildo for? Ya'll don't know huh? Really? Ya'll can't be that slow!"

"We know what they for! You want to fuck us with them right? Duh! We know all that dude! Why don't you try telling us something we don't know?"

They all drank as the O'Jays, "Backstabbers" knocked in the background. It was the perfect time to toss a curveball in their direction.

"Them dildos to fuck alright!"

"And?"

"But I don't want to fuck ya'll with them. I was thinking more like ya'll fucking me with them! Now that's something ya'll didn't know!"

Racquel spit the liquor out upon hearing his warped request. Cake said nothing. She drank more tequila as her friend tried her best to regain her composure. You don't want to offend/insult a man who you just witnessed throwing another man in the trunk over who knows what.

"So let me get this right. You want to be fucked with the strap on? Is that correct?" Cake asked.

"That is absolutely correct. You got a problem with that?"

"I ain't got a problem with nothing but being broke nigga! I ain't tripping!" Cake said putting on the fugazi dick.

Mark took his robe off to expose his bad built, naked body. The smile on his face let them know that this was not his first time to the checkout line.

"Girl you gone fuck him in his ass?" Racquel whispered.

"I sure in the shit am! What's your problem bitch? Quit acting all scary and shit!"

"Bitch I ain't scared of shit! I'm just not seeing the logic in this shit here! This shit is beyond freaked out for me!"

Cake laughed as she greased up the fake dick. Mark got on the couch and waited to be mounted from behind. He had something in the crack of his anus that could not be ignored. That caught their attention quickly.

"What you got in your ass already?" Racquel blurted with zero shame in her tone.

"Oh? That's those balls you put up there for safe keeping you hear me?" Mark laughed.

"This real freak shit bitch! They either loosen your asshole or make you cum harder as you pull them out."

"Pull them out? What the fuck you talking about?"

"If you fucking a bitch in her pussy, you have these stuffed up her dooky hole. When she about to cum, you start to pull these out one by one. It supposed to make you cum harder too," Cake explained as she greased the strap on for the task at hand.

"You just gone just stand there or you gone get in the action? Either get in or get gone!" Mark told Racquel.

"Shit! What you want me to do?" Racquel said as she threw her hands up.

Cake moved closer to Mark who was still in the receiving position via doggy style. She squirted some lube in the crack of his hairy anus. He tooted his ass higher in the air. Cake grabbed the first ball on the string and began to pull. One by one, they popped out his ass. He closed his eyes and bit his bottom lip. Racquel looked on at this mind blowing scene. She couldn't wrap her head around it all. The last ball fell and she stuck a finger in to test his temperature. When he didn't budge, she added another digit.

"You like that? You a nasty lil bitch!" Cake said.

She was taunting Mark as she worked his most sacred hole.

"That is what I'm talking about! Bitch I hope you not getting cold feet on me!" Mark said.

"Fuck you mean? I'm trying to get this here ready. Calm the fuck down."

"I ain't calming shit down! That's what the strap on for! I don't get off on no damn fingers! You acting scared as a virgin at a gangbang!"

"Spread them cheeks open then! You doing all that damn talking! Let's get to it then!"

Racquel sat and watched them go back and forth about some illicit ass play. It was as if she was somewhat trapped in a sick ass dream. It was one that there was no waking up from. Mark's ass was shiny and dribbling lube onto the couch. He was holding his cheeks open with both hands. Cake inched a little closer to his waiting hole. She lined the strap on up with his brown eye. She winked at Racquel before inserting the plastic dick head into his bung hole. Mark bit the couch as she dove farther into him.

"Oooh shit girl! Take it easy back there! It ain't like I get down like this every day! Fuck! That shit feeling good! Come here Racquel! Get a little closer to us!" Mark demanded.

She walked over to him. As soon as she got near, he yanked her panties down far enough to get to it. He took his finger and swiped her honey hole. Then he smelled it before licking it.

"Mmmm! This pussy tastes edible. Come and put your leg up on this sofa."

She propped her leg up to give him a better view of her juicy snatch. He opened her lips to expose the clit. He dabbed his tongue on it before licking wildly on her. He ran his finger across her box to get her juices flowing more. He had no problem jabbing his tongue in and out of her trembling twat. She threw her head back and damn near lost her footing on the couch.

"Be careful baby. I got you. Rub that pussy in my face so I can get you all over me! Mmmm! You taste so good!"

"Mmmmm! Do I? What I taste like nigga?" Racquel asked as she polished his face.

Cake slid in and out of his ass while watching him devour Racquel before her eyes. That made her pussy get even warmer. That sensation prompted her to pump his rump with more force. She was working that strap on half way before diving all the way in his rectum. Cake bit her own lip as she slammed his ass.

"Damn bitch! You trying to touch my lungs or something? Fuck! You funky hoe you!"

"Shut the fuck up! Eat on that good pussy right there! Let me handle this here! Hear me nigga? You better keep them cheeks wide open!"

Mark grabbed his cheeks tighter as she punished his Hershey highway. The girls caught eye contact with one another. The shock and uneasy look on Raquel's face caused Cake to smile. She winked at Racquel in hopes of settling her nerves. Racquel just shook her head and closed her eyes. Her mouth hung open with the fire head she was getting from Mark. Her eyes rolled around like loose marbles. Cake was steady pounding his ass from behind.

"Fuck yeah bitch! You doing your thing! Goddamn that shit feels good!"

Cake paid attention to how he was eating Racquel. Her pussy was getting jealous. She wanted to be licked on too. She decided not to rock the boat. Judging by Racquel's face/body, that cream was now on the way. Mark ate her like a hot piece of crispy chicken. His face was so far in that it looked as if she was giving birth to a full grown man.

"Eat that pussy nigga! You know what to do with that tongue huh? Fuck! You about to make me rain all over you face! Is that what you want? You ready to taste my sweet juice?" Racquel asked.

She grabbed the back of his head to press his face further into her sweet pocket. Mark couldn't answer with his mouth full of cat. He just shook his head to let her know that he agreed with every word she spoke. He eased a finger in and out her slippery cunt. That caused her body to tense up for what was coming down her slushy spout.

"Oh my god! You eating my pussy so good right now! Fuck you doing boy? Mmmm! I'm about to bust all over your tongue! You ready for that? Huh? Just like that! Fuck yeah!" Racquel squealed.

The harder Cake stroked him, the more intense his sucking/licking became. It was a three-way going off with only one hitch. Cake was not being satisfied and she wanted in. As soon as her friend achieved an orgasm, she would not be waiting much longer.

"Mmmm! Huh! Fuck! I'm about to spray this shit all in your mouth! Right there! Don't you fucking move!"

Mark bore down on her swollen clit as his finger went crazy on her fuck box. Cake slow grinded in order to not disturb the action. She was thinking about her turn which happened to be fast approaching.

"Cum lil bitch! Let that shit go! You know you want to! Come on and do what you came to do! Hear me lil bitch?" He asked.

He continued to snake his tongue all around the opening of her pussy. That alone was driving her up the exposed brick wall she was leaning against. Racquel closed her eyes and concentrated on the head she was getting that was killing her softly. She could not believe the sensation that his mouth provided. She held his head and her pussy gripped his tongue. The top was about to blow off this boiling pot. Her peak was about to be reached at any moment. Her grip on Mark's head tightened as her nut came on down.

"Ah! Shit nigga! Ohhh! You sucking the shit out of my pussy! Fuck! I'm about to cum boy! Goddamn you cock sucking ass nigga you! Fuck! Shit!" Racquel exhaled as her entire body weakened.

Cake pulled the dick out of Mark's rump and decided it was time to switch up. She smacked his ass as she pulled the synthetic dick from her waist. Her pussy was moist, but she wanted the attention of a tongue also.

"Aye! Put this on and finish up what I started back here. I need some head my damn self! Shit! Here you go!" Cake said.

She handed the strap on to Racquel. Mark switched his position on the couch to allow better access to his greedy asshole. He got on his back and threw his legs back in the buck position. Racquel applied more lube to the artificial cock. She squirted more into his open ass. Cake squatted over his face and he went to work on her just like he did her friend.

"Damn that mouth serious! You ain't tell me it was like this girl!"

"Shit! I figured you wanted to see for yourself. That shit stupid fire ain't it?" Racquel asked.

She lined the cock up with his shitter as Cake rode his face. Racquel eased up in his ass with a slowed down stroke. Her legs were still shaking from her orgasmic episode. Mark's legs hung in the air as he began to stroke his own dick. He spit on his hands in order to reduce the friction of skin to skin action. Racquel shook her head at the nigga who she was scared to get next to just a few hours ago. Now she had a cock in his booty. Funny how shit goes sometimes.

"Fuck that ass like that nigga owe you child support! Don't take it easy on him! All that shit he was talking? Girl you better get with his ass! Literally! Fuck this nigga ass up!" Cake cheered her on.

"She scared of this shit here! You see the look on her face? She ain't with this shit for real! Her pussy got a sweet taste to it though! Sweet, scary pussy ass bitch!" Mark teased.

Racquel listened to them both. There were right about her. She had never been in a situation such as this before. Shit was fucking her whole understanding up for sure. Seeing a so called hard ass goon getting treated like a bitch was something that she never wanted to get used to seeing. She was taking it light on him until they both began to mock her. Her disgust eventually transformed into disdain. She peered down and took it out on Mark's doo doo maker. Her pelvic thrusts became faster and more intense.

"Ah shit! Goddamn hoe! You mad at me or something? Goddamn! What the fuck?"

Racquel didn't respond. She pumped away on him like a possessed demon. Cake oscillated on Mark's mug to get a closer look at the action. She grabbed his ankles and stretched them as far backwards as they could go. Mark started tongue fucking Cake's ass. He was jacking his cock even faster. Cake spat on his dick to assist in a smoother jack. She looked at Racquel who had a grimace on her face that let you know that business was being handled. Cake smirked and nodded to her. She expanded her butt and bounced on his face seductively. Racquel spilled more lube to ensure that the action was not interrupted.

"Yeah! Eat that ass nigga! Fuck yeah! I love this here! Gots to appreciate a nasty mufucka! Ooooh! Shit yeah! Keep that damn tongue flicking nigga! Ooooh yeah! Goddamn!"

Racquel started pulling half way out and then jabbing it right back in. She repeated this agenda over again to let him feel her in the worst way. A couple of farts escaped his orifice as the air built up inside of him.

"Damn nigga! You gassing and shit! Hold that shit down you nasty mufucka!" Cake stated fake mugging at him.

"Shut up! Blame your home girl for that! She the reason! Hear me?"

Racquel had a slight, half ass grin on her face. Plugging his ass was starting to give her an adrenaline rush. The energy crammed in the room was nothing short of bizarre. Cake fingered her snatch with a tongue up her rump. She winked at Racquel who winked back. That allowed them both to know that they were now and always would be on the same page in the same book. The O'Jays "Backstabbers" played on the system. The aroma in the area was hard to ignore. They were definitely playing in deep water. It was good that they were excellent swimmers though! All that alcohol was catching up. Racquel was becoming nauseated. The room began to rotate and tilt along with her stomach. Before she knew it, everything that was once down was now on its way back up and out of her mouth. Mark's chest was the unlikely target.

"Aaargh! Ooooh! Whoooa! Aaaargh!" She heaved all over him.

"Oh shit! Girl you alright? What the? Shit!" Cake said as she watched her friend upchuck several times more.

You would think that that would be enough to send Mark into a frenzy but it wasn't. He just kept on jacking his cock off. Cake dismounted from Mark's face to help her friend to the lavatory. Racquel continued to vomit throughout the house.

"Girl come your ass on! Goddamn it! Your ass puking like a fool! You done threw up all over that freak ass nigga! Put your head all the way in that toilet! Shit that shit stank! Damn girl! You know you can't be drinking like that! You have to know your ledge bitch!"

"I know right! I was trying to take my mind off of what was going on. I ain't never done no shit like that before girl! What the fuck! That's a different type of nigga right there! Goddamn that shit was crazy!" Racquel said in between gags.

Cake held her around the waist and rubbed her back. She heaved for another five minutes before standing up. She checked herself in the mirror. Her eyes were bloodshot. There was caked up remnants of upchuck all around her mouth.

"Damn girl! My face looking all sorts of messed up girl! Let me wash my damn face off right quick! Give me some of that mouthwash!" Racquel said in a hoarse tone.

She gargled and spit several times. She cleaned her face and stood there for a few seconds. She was so fucked up that she hadn't noticed that she still had the make believe dick on.

"Girl! Look at me! Why I got this bitch still on? Answer me that girl!" Racquel laughed at herself.

"Damn girl I was too busy trying to get you together that I hadn't even noticed! Hell nah! That is crazy as fuck!" Cake added.

She pulled it off and left it on the bathroom floor. She took one more swig from the mouthwash bottle. She wiped her face and then her pussy. Cake washed hers also. They finished up and walked back downstairs. Anita Baker's "Rapture" was playing. They started dancing and putting their clothes back on. Mark rose up from the couch when he peeped them.

"Fuck ya'll doing? Da fuck going on? What's up?"

"We about to bounce out. We'll clean your spot up before we go through. Don't even trip dude. We got you," Cake said with a wink.

"Da fuck you is! I don't need ya'll to clean up shit in this mufucka! Where the fuck that strap at?"

"What strap?" Racquel answered thinking he was referring to a pistol.

"The strap on bitch! Your puking ass went to the bathroom with it still on! The shit ain't around your waist no more! What the fuck ya'll on? I ain't through fucking and neither are ya'll! Fuck you mean?" Mark shouted over the music.

His upper body was still covered in vomit. The girls had their clothes on by now. They stood side by side as he clowned them. He was still drinking out the bottle so he was good and blasted.

"Nigga! We done with this here! Now if you want to pick this up at a later time, so be it. We about to pop out and get in traffic. Catch you later dude cause you talking crazy as shit right now," Cake said matter of factly.

That attitude only incensed Mark more. His eyes damn near jumped from his skull.

"Huh? Who you talking to? Bitch ya'll ain't done until I say ya'll done!" Mark yelled.

"Dude let us out since you don't need any help cleaning up the mess we made. Don't try to say we didn't offer to help. I'll hit you as soon as you cool off. Hear me nigga? We up!" Cake said firmly.

The sight of him covered in puke with a semi hard cock was beyond words. On top of it all, he had a fucking attitude. The girls walked to the door slowly. They kept an eye on Mark at the same time. He closed in on them as they reached for the door knob.

"Well fuck ya'll fake ass hoes! Fuck you all up your asses! Hoes be gone! Get the fuck outta here!" He screamed at them.

Cake couldn't believe her eyes let alone her ears.

"This nigga fronting on us like that? Da fuck wrong with him? He out of order for real!" Cake thought to herself.

She turned to face him since he was on her heels.

"Now listen here mufucka! You ain't just gone keep spitting garbage out your mouth where me and my girl are concerned! Now you going too far! We are about to go before shit gets even more out of hand! Holla at you whenever since you got an attitude like your period just came!"

Mark squinted his eyes and tightened his mouth. He balled up his fists like he was about to swing on them. They zeroed in on his dick beaters that he now had posed as weapons.

"Fuck ya'll then! Ya'll wasn't on shit no way! You ain't got to call me with your fake asses!"

"Fake? Who you calling fake? Nigga we been real from jump with your sick ass! How you gone fix your mouth to say that?" Cake said.

"We about to slide on out. Sorry you feel that way dude. We appreciate your hospitality," Racquel said.

She was trying her best to diffuse the situation. She placed herself in between her friend and Mark. Cake stepped out the door with Mark still standing in the doorway. Racquel turned to follow her friend to the car. Mark mushed her in the back of the head.

"Man what the fuck is your problem? You ain't got to be putting your hands on nobody!"

"Girl he just mad that we tired of playing his twisted ass game! You mad big baby? Fuck out of here with that sensitive ass bullshit!"

Faint kicks and cries could be heard from the trunk of Mark's car. Both girls looked in the direction of the whip and neither could believe their ears.

"Bitch do you hear that?" Racquel asked softly.

"Of course I do bitch! This crazy mufucka still got dude in his fucking trunk!" Cake whispered.

"Get your stupid asses on then! I was done fucking with ya'll tired asses anyway! Fuck outta here! Dumb ass hoes!" He yelled.

"Dumb? You the one just got fucked up your ass by two bitches with the same dick! You want the dick so bad? Go get the mufucka up off the bathroom floor and fuck your damn self! Hear me bitch? Or better yet, why don't you free this nigga from your trunk so he can finish the job!"

Upon hearing that, Mark ran back into the house and left the door wide open. They were certain that he was going to get a gun. They both took off running and laughing to the car.

"Girl start this bitch so we can get away from here!" Cake said shutting the door.

Racquel cranked up the ride and they pulled away from the curb. Halfway down the street, they heard gunshots. When they looked back, Mark was running down the street shooting at them.

"Girl this nigga shooting at us! Get the fuck outta here!"

A bullet shattered their back window while another one cracked one of their side view mirrors. She pressed a lil harder on the gas as they turned the corner. Cake fired up another exotic blunt to calm her nerves. She continued to go through her missed texts.

"Girl fuck these niggas! They ain't who they portray for real! Look at that bullshit back there! We met him kidnapping a mufucka! Then we go to fuck with him and he wants to get his ass fucked! Now what kind of shit is that? We are living in some fucked up times!"

"Why you say that girl?"

"I say that because the niggas want to be bitches and these bitches want to be niggas! Flip flop ass shit! It's funny to me. I don't know how to be no one but me."

Cake's words hung in the air along with the Kush smoke. The ladies laughed it off; but were very much thankful to be alive.

You're The Publisher, We're Your Legs

Crystell Publications is not your publisher, but we will help you self-publish your own novel. **We Offer Editing For An Extra Fee, and Highly Suggest It, If Waived, We Print What You Submit!**

Don't have all your money? …. No Problem!
Ask About our Payment Plans

Crystal Perkins-Stell, MHR
Essence Magazine Bestseller
We Give You Books!
PO BOX 8044 / Edmond – OK 73083
www.crystalstell.com
(405) 414-3991

Hey! Stop Wishing and get your book to print NOW!!!

$674.00 Spring POD Special 250 page Manuscript. **Add $75.00** for custom covers. 2 Proofs –Publisher & Printer Copy, Mink Magazine Subscription, Free Advertisement, Book Cover, ISBN #, Conversion, Typeset, Correspondence, Masters, 8 hrs Consultation.   ***Inquire about our 100 book plan rates**

Grind Plans 25 & E-Book Order Extra Books	Hustle Hard $899.00 255-275pg	Respect The Code $869.00 250 -205	313 Deal $839.00 200 -80
Insanity Plans E-Book & POD Extra Books Can Be Ordered	Psycho $759.00 225-250pg	Spastic $659.00 200-220	Mental $559.00 70pgs or less
All Manuscript Options except the E-Books include: 2 Proofs–Printer, Mink Magazine Subscription, Free Advertisement, Book Cover, ISBN #, Conversion, Typeset, Correspondence, Masters, 8 hrs Consultation			

$100.00 E-book upload only
$275.00-Book covers/Authors input
$200.00-Book covers/ templates
$190.00 and up Websites
$175.00 and up, book trailers

$75 Can't afford edits, Spell-check
$499 Flat Rate Edits Exceeds 210 add 1.50
$200-Typeset Book Format PDF File
$200 and up / Type Manuscript Call for details
$1.60 Per Page to Type

We're Changing The Game.
No more paying Vanity Presses $8 to $10 per book! We Give You Books @ Cost.